Highland Quest

Judy Allen

RED FOX

Judy Allen has written over 30 published titles. She has won the Earthworm Award, the Whitbread Children's Novel Award and been Commended for the Carnegie Medal.

Quest Tours and Travel is a fictitious company and all the characters in this book are fictional.

A Red Fox Book

Published by Random House Children's Books
20 Vauxhall Bridge Road, London SW1V 2SA

A division of Random House UK Ltd
London Melbourne Sydney Auckland
Johannesburg and agencies throughout the world

1 3 5 7 9 10 8 6 4 2

First published simultaneously in hardback and paperback by
Julia MacRae and Red Fox 1996

Set in Plantin by Intype London Ltd

Printed and bound in Great Britain by
Cox & Wyman Ltd, Reading, Berkshire

RANDOM HOUSE UK Limited Reg. No. 954009

ISBN 0 09 965111 4

CONTENTS

For Jean

CHAPTER ONE

Highland Flyers

"I think I've just seen a sparrow-harrier," said Ruth. "But now all I'm getting is sky."

"Binoculars can be very tricky if you're not used to them," said my mother.

"So can bird names," I said. "You've just invented the sparrow-harrier. It must have been either a sparrow-hawk or a hen-harrier."

My father was struggling a bit, with one foot deep in a boggy patch. He heaved it free with a hideous sucking sound. "In actual fact," he said, "it was a buzzard."

The four of us were walking over a piece of damp moorland. The piece of damp moorland was in the Scottish Borders. This meant that it was cold, in spite of the spring sunshine, and rather bleak.

I have to say I'd been quite anxious about Ruth when we set out. I wasn't sure how a New Yorker would react to all this empty scenery. Although she's lived in London for years, ever since her American mother married her English step-father, this was the first time she'd ever been to Scotland, which was surprising.

It was also the first time she'd been on a trip with my family, which was not so surprising. My parents almost never go away.

My mother runs Quest Tours – 'Holidays for People who are Seeking Something'. She travels a lot for work. Travel is not something she wants to do with her free time.

My father runs Quest Travel, which sells Quest Tours and also all kinds of other tours and trips and tickets. He says a holiday isn't a holiday to him. Especially if there are strangers doing the same thing in the same place.

Just occasionally, though, something gets them moving. This time it was a small advert in the newspaper. My father saw it in the travel section, which normally he only reads for research purposes. It was a special offer – a long weekend in a farmhouse at a really good price. What was crucial, though, was that it ended with the magic words 'excellent bird-watching country'.

Suddenly, we were in the car heading north for Dumfriesshire.

I think Dad likes bird-watching the way some people like fishing. It gives him an excuse to go somewhere lonely and stare into space. To be fair, though, he can get quite enthusiastic. Once, when he thought he'd spotted a firecrest up an oak tree, he brought the binoculars up so fast he blacked both his eyes.

I like bird-watching, too, but somehow I hadn't expected Ruth to find it appealing.

Here she was, though, one hand holding her hair back, the other gripping a pair of borrowed bins, staring at a disappearing dot in the sky and saying, "Okay. So can I claim to have seen a buzzard? Even though I didn't know what it was?"

My father bent down and pointed to a small, boring plant, half-hidden in the grass. "What's that?" he said.

Ruth examined it carefully. "I have absolutely no idea," she said eventually.

"Neither have I," said my father. "But whatever it is, we've definitely both seen it."

"I think that was a 'yes' to your buzzard question," said my mother. "I also think it's time to start back."

"Right," said Ruth. "Do we get to do this again tomorrow?"

"Do you want to?" I said.

"Sure."

"Do you mean that, or are you just being polite?"

"Jo!" said Ruth. "How long have you known me? Am I ever polite?"

We only had one more day away. Then it was back to reality for all of us.

Ruth and I are both taking a year out between school and college. I have to admit it isn't turning out exactly as we expected – though bits of it have been really good. The idea was to work and earn, save and plan, then travel and party.

I got a job at once, as a dogsbody for Quest. I would like to point out, here, that this only sounds like an easy option to people who have never worked for my parents.

Ruth, though, has had really bad luck. It's been hard for her to find jobs, and when she has, they haven't lasted. And it's never been her fault. I mean, it genuinely hasn't been her fault. So she never has much money. Which is a pity because wherever you want to travel, you have to pay.

Unless you're my parents, of course.

It was on the walk back to the farm that they began to discuss free holidays. Gloomily. Which I have to say I thought was very tactless of them.

First, my father sympathised with my mother about hotel managers who offered her a room for nothing in the hope she'd include them in a Quest Tour. Then my mother sympathised with my father about tour operators who offered a no-charge away-break to encourage him to sell their excursions through the Quest Travel shop.

"People think of them as perks," said Mum, who wears out suitcases the way other people wear out shoes. "But it's just another part of the job."

"I skip mine," said Dad, who only takes his pass-port out of the filing cabinet when his photo needs updating.

Later, Ruth said she'd more or less guessed right then what was going to happen. I hadn't. I was too busy being indignant at the waste. I didn't begin to get ideas until that evening when my mother took the call from the Quest Tours Office.

"Problems?" said my father.

"Just Bill panicking. He's trying to set something up for a client and he can't find enough information on file. I had to tell him it isn't there because we haven't got hold of it yet. Or not much of it, anyway."

We'd walked all day. We'd eaten heavily in the farmhouse kitchen. Now we were slumped round the fire in the guest sitting room, staring into the flames. No one had the energy to respond at once.

"Important client?" I said, after a peaceful silence.

"They're all important," said my mother automatically. "This one's a Canadian called James MacDonald. He wants to find his Scottish ancestors."

"I guess there's a lot to be said for family reunions with dead people," said Ruth. She was idly twisting some of her hair into a plait. "You'd know they weren't going to pick fights with you or be rude about your clothes."

"It isn't like Quest," I said, "to be late with information."

"He was booked onto the Quest for Ancestors Tour last month," said my mother. "But he missed it. He was staying with his daughter in France, on the way here, and he got ill. So he cancelled and booked himself onto next year's tour instead. Naturally I told the researcher not to bother with him till nearer the time. I should have foreseen what could happen."

"What did?"

"He got better and decided he couldn't bear to go straight back to Canada without seeing the land of his forefathers. He's still going to do the proper tour next year, but he'd like to do a mini-tour this year. Bill thought he could set something up, but Fiona hadn't got far before I stopped her and she hasn't time to do anything in the next couple of days."

Ruth finished plaiting the lock of hair and let go of it. It hung straight down between her eyes, along her nose, across her mouth and ended up some way below her chin. Because her hair is so long and wild and red, I thought she meant it to do that. Two seconds later she began to unplait it again, and I realised she didn't.

"Fortunately," my mother went on, "we do know his grandfather was head deer keeper at Inverhaig Castle. Even more fortunately, the castle is now a hotel, so Bill's booked him a room. That should keep him on the boil till next year."

"Inverhaig?" said my father. "Tumbleweed goes there."

"Excuse me?" said Ruth, abandoning the new plait she'd just started on.

"Tumbleweed Themed Tours," said my father. "I do pretty well by them. Sell them in handfuls. They're desperate to give me and my 'partner' two days on one of their jaunts. I don't think they've twigged that my partner runs a rival company."

My mother looked thoughtful. "Is there any chance they'll be at Inverhaig when Mr MacDonald's there?" she said. "In two days' time?"

"Quite likely. It's on one of their well-worn tracks."

"If they are, it might be worth taking them up on their offer," said Mum. "Just for once, a freebie could be useful."

"Could you plug into a tour just like that?" I said. "At such short notice?"

"Can't answer your question without checking," said my father, "but I know they'd do their best to accommodate us. They'd see it as good business strategy."

"Obviously it has to be meant," said Ruth. "Doesn't it? The free offer and the free-wheeling client coming together like that?"

"I admit I'd be quite interested to see a Tumble-weed Tour from the inside," said my mother thoughtfully. "And Mr MacDonald has just retired, so he could well become a regular client." Then she shook her head. "I need to get back to London," she said. "I have meetings I can't cancel."

"Where is Inverhaig Castle Hotel?" I said.

"It's in the Highlands," said my mother. She looked at me as if she'd only just realised I was in the room. "I suppose you and Ruth . . ." She raised her eyebrows questioningly at my father.

"Don't see why not," he said. "Jo does work for Quest, after all. They should accept that. And I'd be willing to give her a bit more time off, if you would."

"As it's my client she'd be looking after," said Mum, "I think I'd have to." She smiled at us. "And I think we should remember Jo and Ruth have done well for both branches of Quest in the past."

"Very true," said Dad. "Well, it's up to you high-flyers. Shall I go and make the call?"

A few minutes earlier I had been nearly asleep in the glow of the fire. Now I was extremely awake. "I definitely don't think we should leave a client wandering around unattended," I said. "We could probably find some more information for him while we're up there."

Ruth gave me one of her straight looks. "Stand back," she said. "Jo's getting into tour-guide mode. I can tell."

"There *is* supposed to be a diary or something at Inverhaig," said Mum. "We haven't followed up on it, but you could have a word with someone while

7

you're there. And there should be family graves in the local churchyard."

I could feel enthusiasm building up in me. It's partly that I really do like sorting things out. Mostly, though, it's that I cling to the hope that if I use my initiative often enough my parents will give me more interesting things to do. I know they probably won't. I know they really need someone to do all the menial stuff, and I know they can't afford to employ anyone else. Even so, I still like to try for it.

"Will the hotel have a fax?" I said.

"Hey, big city woman," said Ruth. "Are you saying you won't go unless it's a high-tech-digital-stereo-fibre-optic-internet wonderland, or what?"

"I was just thinking," I said, in my most dignified voice, "that there's obviously *some* information back at the office. So Bill could fax it through for me."

Dad heaved himself to his feet. "Jo seems to be up for it," he said. "How about you, Ruth?"

"I don't have any major commitments in the next few days," said Ruth. "On account of being out of work. Again."

Dad nodded and headed off towards the phone.

"Now let me get this clear," said Ruth. "Is Mr MacDonald with Tumbleweed Tours or Quest Tours?"

"With Quest," said Mum. "But he's travelling alone. Tumbleweed clearly hasn't taken over the whole hotel or Bill couldn't have got him a room."

"If Dad can't get us on this freebie," I said, "should we book ourselves into Inverhaig anyway? It isn't the tour that matters, is it? It's being on hand for Mr MacDonald."

Mum shook her head. "Quest couldn't justify the expense," she said. "Not for just one client."

Ruth sighed. "The Highlands," she said dreamily. "Sounds romantic, doesn't it?"

"Don't get too excited," I said. "The Tumbleweed Tour may not be due at Inverhaig at the same time as Mr MacD. And even if it is, there may not be space on it for us."

"It will," said Ruth. "And there will. I've seen this before. Once you decide to use your initiative, nothing stops you."

My father came back into the room. Ruth didn't ask about the result of the phone call. She just said, "What *is* this Tour we're about to gatecrash? You said it was 'Themed'. What's the Theme?"

Dad looked across at Mum and grinned. "It's one you tried, once," he said. "But you withdrew it from the brochure quite quickly. You said it was definitely more trouble than it was worth, I remember."

"Hit me with it," said Ruth.

"It's a tour called Haunted Britain," said Dad. "Apparently Inverhaig Castle has ghosts. Or so the publicity leaflet says, anyway."

CHAPTER TWO

The Cinder Inn

"You know what," said Ruth, gazing out of the train window. "I don't think I approve of ghosts."

She had been right about the way things had turned out, of course. The two-week Haunted Britain Tour *was* due to overlap with Mr MacDonald's visit by one night. And Tumbleweed *had* tumbled over themselves to let us share in forty-eight hours of it without charge.

What was more, the farm's office had had a fax, so maps, brochures and information had slithered through at us from Tumbleweed and from Bill back at Quest.

As a result, my parents' car was heading south without us. At the same time, we were heading north, without very much idea of what we were supposed to do when we got there.

"I could understand you being *frightened* of ghosts," I said. "But how can you disapprove of them?"

I wondered if Ruth might be having doubts about the trip. She often does, I've noticed. Especially if she's been taken by surprise and rushed into something.

"Well they're selfish, aren't they?" she said.

"I don't follow you."

"A ghost was once alive, right? It knows what it's like to be human, okay? So – it has to be aware that if it wanders around in the night, transparent and moaning and giving off a smell of rotting flesh, it's going to terrify people. Yeah?"

"I suppose so."

"Well then why does it do it? Because it's self-centred, that's why! If it had any consideration at all it'd wraith around somewhere private where it wouldn't be noticed."

"When you really think about it," I said, "not *that* many people say they've seen ghosts. Perhaps most of them do keep a low profile."

"They're okay then," said Ruth. "What an ex-person does in the privacy of its own tomb is its own business."

"You're not usually so judgmental," I said. "Anyway, what if a ghost doesn't want to haunt? What if it can't help it?"

"There have been times," said Ruth severely, "when I haven't been able to help throwing up. But I have always managed to do it where no one else could see."

"That's different."

"No it isn't. They're both unexpected out-of-the-body activities. And from what your mother said, I think she feels the same way I do."

"Not exactly. She set up a Quest for Haunted Europe tour once."

"Yes, but she withdrew it, didn't she? She said so."

"The first one went ahead. It ended up in Transylvania. Though I don't think Dracula is strictly a ghost."

"You mean there really *is* a place called Transylvania?"

"Of course. It's in Romania."

"I never knew that!" said Ruth. "So what went wrong? Did everyone get bitten by rabid bats, or what?"

"Nothing went wrong. Mum just lost her nerve. She started to worry about lawsuits. She said if the clients didn't get a fright they might want their money back. And if they did they could sue for post-spook trauma. She decided the financial risk was too high."

"That makes sense," said Ruth. "So how do Tumbleweed Themed Tours get around that little number?"

"I'm happy to say that's their problem."

"Maybe they only go places where haunting is guaranteed."

It's amazing how long you can know someone without ever having certain conversations.

"You *are* joking?" I said.

Ruth just looked at me.

"We don't believe in ghosts," I said. "Do we?"

"You speak for yourself," said Ruth. She rapped on the train window. "Look at that. There's more going on out there than meets the eye. Isn't there?"

The scenery had been getting steadily more spectacular with each mile. At first, the mountains had simply stood around, looking picturesque. Now, though, they were definitely beginning to loom.

The snow on the tops was sparkling prettily, but when I looked at the dark, craggy lower slopes I had to admit they did have a haunted look about them.

"It's dramatic," I said cautiously. "I'll give you that."

"We couldn't survive up there for long. Not without a packload of equipment and a regular supply drop."

"That's all right, we don't have to."

"But the mountains *know* that," said Ruth with relish. "And so do the spirits of all the people who've died up there."

Fortunately, the train began to slow down for our station and this stopped the conversation.

It isn't exactly that I don't believe in ghosts. It's more that I don't *want* to believe in ghosts. In fact I don't even want to think about ghosts. I work on the assumption that if I don't give them any attention, they won't give me any, either.

"You mean we actually get out here?" said Ruth, as I stood up. "I was beginning to think this journey would go on for the rest of my life."

I knew how she felt.

First, my parents had driven us to the station at Dumfries so we could travel by rail up to Glasgow.

At Glasgow we'd changed onto a train that had brought us right up into the Highlands.

Now we had to catch a postbus which would take us a few kilometres further and drop us outside a small hotel. A very small hotel. Not much more than a pub, probably. There we would be collected by the Tumbleweed tour bus as it passed by on its way from Glamis to Inverhaig.

Or that was the plan, anyway.

Short of hiring a car, which would have been expensive, it was the simplest way of getting where we were going.

"I do wonder why I'm doing this," said Ruth, as we climbed off the train. "My introduction to bird-watching is over. I should be home, looking for work."

I hooked my back-pack over one shoulder and walked out to the front of the station. "The postbus should be along in ten minutes," I said. "I'm glad the train wasn't late. The timing's a bit tight."

Ruth followed me. "I'd forgotten how much I hate carrying my luggage," she said, dumping her pack on the ground at her feet. "What with two trains and all those stations, you'd think someone might have had the courtesy to steal it."

"You didn't like it when you lost it in Amsterdam," I said.

"It was a lot easier to get to Amsterdam," said Ruth. "In fact I think it's easier to get to New York. This is such a tiny island! How come we have to take a car, two trains and then a bus! Why can't I just shut my eyes and say 'Beam me up, Scottie'?"

"Because this is reality. You can't step into a magic capsule and – *boomph* – you're there."

"Yeah, you can," said Ruth. "It's called a plane."

"Planes cost money."

"I didn't want to buy one. I just thought it'd be nice to fly in one."

"That only works if there's an airport where you want to go."

Ruth looked up and down the road. "Is there a

café we can wait in?" she said. "I don't want to sound as if I'm complaining, or anything, but it's cold out here."

But there wasn't a café. There wasn't even a tea-bar in the station, which was very small.

It wouldn't get dark for at least another hour, but the sky was covered in thick grey cloud which gave a good imitation of dusk. There was a slight wind, which was more than slightly chilly, and I suspected I'd just felt a drop of rain.

"I've got chocolate in my pack," I said. "Do you want some?"

"It's okay, I'll wait. We get dinner at this hotel, don't we?"

"Certainly do."

"Right," said Ruth. "Here's the story. We dine by candlelight in the Great Hall where we both meet stunning Highlanders and fall desperately in love over the Scotch broth. I could do with some romance."

"What would Gareth say!"

"This will just be a short interlude followed by heartbreak," said Ruth. "It won't affect on-going relationships. Anyhow, for all I know Gareth's met a rich ski-kid in France."

She said it very casually, but I knew how she felt. She and Gareth have been together for more than a year. While he was supermarket-shelf-stacking and she was in and out of work locally, they saw each other most days. Then he got an offer of a three-month job as a chalet-maid in a ski resort in the French Pyrenees. Ruth told him it was a chance he shouldn't miss. And she meant it. But that didn't mean she wasn't worried.

"I think Gareth's the faithful type," I said. "But I know what you mean."

Ruth gave me a quick hug. "Sorry, Jo," she said. "It's worse for you and Tom."

"Not worse. Just different. My fault for getting involved with someone who lives on the other side of the world. Let's talk about something more cheerful."

"Scottish talent!" said Ruth. "Guys in skirts. A ghost-hunter on the Tumbleweed Tour maybe."

"Don't get your hopes up. They'll probably all be grey panthers."

"What are you talking about?"

"Retired people."

"Ah. Rich old dudes who can afford to go travelling. Got you. But first we have to get this postbus, right. What *is* a postbus?"

"That is," I said, pointing as a bright red van with a gold crown on its door rolled into sight round the corner.

"Oh, you mean post like in mail," said Ruth. "I was thinking of post like in fence."

"How could you think that?" I said. "It wouldn't make sense."

"There's a lot of stuff in this country that doesn't make sense. I'm used to it."

The van pulled up beside us. The driver jumped out and opened the door for us to get in the back. Then he collected a couple of letters from the post box in the wall outside the station and climbed back behind the wheel.

"So we get delivered with the junk mail," said Ruth, settling herself behind a half open sack full of catalogues. "Fine, I don't have a problem with that."

We had a problem with something else, though. Quite soon.

The driver was friendly and cheerful – until I told him where we would like him to drop us off. The news seemed to depress him.

"You're clearly strangers here," he said. "I could take you on to a nice wee town, if you like. Just a few miles further north."

"No, we definitely want to get off at that pub or hotel or whatever it is," I said. "It is on your route, isn't it?"

"Aye, it is one of my stops," he said. "I just hope you weren't planning to stay over."

"Why?" said Ruth. "Is it haunted?"

"Not so far as I know," said the driver. "But it is closed down."

The van rattled along the empty road at an impressive speed. The driver said no more.

"We're just meeting some people outside it," I said, feeling I wanted to reassure him. "So we must go there."

"You know your own business best, I'm sure," he said. "Here we are."

And sure enough, there we were.

The pub stood alone, in empty countryside. There was no sign of a house or a shop or a petrol station or anything else nearby.

In fact there was nothing in the visible landscape except us, the pub and the postbus.

That would have been unnerving enough for two city-dwellers. What made it worse, though, was that the pub had not just closed down. It had also burnt down. Right down. To the ground. All that was left were two blackened gable ends standing each side of a vast heap of rubble and charcoal.

"You're sure you want me to leave you here?" said the driver.

Ruth was temporarily speechless.

At first I thought I was, too. Then I drew a deep breath. "Yes, I'm sure," I said, as firmly as I could. "We have an appointment with a coach."

He nodded, waved and drove off.

After that there was nothing in the visible landscape except us and the pub.

"Welcome to the Cinder Inn," said Ruth quietly.

CHAPTER THREE

A Phantom Freebie?

The only thing left standing in the whole burnt-out place was part of the low wall at the front, the wall that had once encircled the car park.

So we sat on that.

The road was empty of traffic in both directions. To the south it disappeared behind a mixture of crags and low cloud. To the north it vanished into damp gloom.

The sky seemed to be losing light by the minute. The air seemed to be gaining moisture by the second.

Ruth summed up our feelings about Tumbleweed Tours.

"What a load of bozos," she said. "How come they didn't know this place had been torched? I wouldn't let a performing cat-flea book with them after this. How long do we have to sit here and get rained on?"

"It isn't real rain," I said. "I think this is what they call Scotch mist."

"Amazingly enough," said Ruth, "that doesn't make it any more attractive. Why couldn't they have picked us up at the station?"

"It's off their route. The coach doesn't pass it."

"So are you saying this coach has no steering wheel?"

"I suppose they could have made a detour."

"Exactly," said Ruth. "Quest would have. I think we should complain."

"I don't know if you can complain when you're on a freebie," I said. "I'm not really sure of the etiquette."

"I see headlights," said Ruth.

She leapt to her feet and stepped out onto the road.

Almost immediately she stepped back again as a ten-wheeled juggernaut rolled past us.

The mist swirled about a bit and then closed in behind it.

Ruth heaved her back-pack onto the wall beside her. "I have a flashlight in here somewhere," she said, unbuckling the front pocket.

"What do you want that for? There's nothing to look at."

"I want it to signal with," said Ruth. "If it's much darker by the time they get here they're never going to see us. They'll just spin right past, like that truck."

I opened my own back-pack and checked with the Useful Information section at the front of my diary.

"Officially," I said, "the sun doesn't set for another forty-five minutes. I think it's just that we're inside a cloud."

"That doesn't make us any more visible," said Ruth, testing her torch.

After about ten minutes, more lights approached. Before we had time to get excited, though, we saw it was only a car.

Ten minutes after that another truck came past.

"When are Tumbleweed due to pick us up?" said Ruth.

"Almost half an hour ago."

Ruth looked over her shoulder at the burnt wreckage behind us. This was something I'd been willing myself not to do ever since I sat down.

"Wow! Will you look at that!" she whispered.

"I'd rather not, thanks," I said.

"Come on!" said Ruth. "We're on a spook-hunting trip, don't forget. A Phantom Freebie. We're *supposed* to be scared! Go with it!"

"We're not on it yet," I said. "And I'm not scared."

I wasn't. Not exactly. It was just that I knew I could easily become scared, if I let myself. As long as I faced the road, and kept my mind on the coach that I was sure must be about to appear at any second, I could stay calm.

In case you think this sounds childish or neurotic, I'd like to point out that it took great strength of mind not to look behind me.

It was Ruth's fault that I gave way. There's a limit to how long you can sit beside someone who is staring and staring at something without finding your head turning itself round automatically.

I can't tell you how horrible that inn looked. Now that the sky really was almost dark, it somehow managed to look bigger than it had before. It also looked closer. The pointed gable ends had become vast witches' hats. The enormous heap of collapsed brick and beams between them was a huge, crouching animal.

What was worse, the more I stared, the more I thought I could see movement amongst the rubble.

I knew it was partly the mist and partly imagination, but somehow that didn't help.

Ruth helped even less. "Are you still saying you don't believe in ghosts?" she said softly.

"I am!" I said, as firmly as I could. "*I* don't believe in them and *you* don't approve of them. So there's no point talking about them. If you must go on about things that don't exist, why can't you choose friendly ones? Like Santa Claus? Or the Tooth Fairy?"

"Have you forgotten my problem with Santa?" said Ruth, turning from the sinister view and staring down the road again. "How I nearly got fired because I refused to be his Little Helper?"

"They wanted you to dress up as a Christmas Angel, that's all. You might have looked quite good."

"What – humiliate myself in a department store where any of my friends might see me?"

"Someone did it."

"And that's why she got a permanent job when the Sales were over and I didn't. I know. I'm sorry but I have my principles. And since you mentioned her, I've disapproved of the Tooth Fairy since I was a kid."

"The *Tooth* Fairy? Why?"

"Why not? Suddenly I was given some weird story about an elf who wanted to buy my teeth. It was horrible. I kept wondering what she planned to do with them."

"You're taking it too seriously. It was just a nice way of giving a child a bit of extra pocket money."

"I decided fairyland must use human teeth instead

of hard currency," said Ruth. "I assumed molars had more value than dollars. I pictured her hanging around, willing my second teeth to fall out as well, so she could afford to upgrade her wand."

I stood up and spun round. "Something *did* move back there," I said.

Ruth gripped my arm. "I know. I heard it," she whispered. "A kind of scrattering noise."

Nothing happened for about ten seconds, except that my heart stopped and the dark ruins beyond the wall seemed to take on even more fantastic and sinister shapes.

Then we heard the sound again, much closer.

Something small, pale and snake-like shot out, almost as if the skeleton of the inn had stuck its tongue out at us.

Without pausing, it rippled past the broken end of our wall, across the road and out of sight.

We couldn't decide exactly what it was. Ruth insisted it was a polecat. I was sure it was a stoat. But we did agree it was a small, harmless, wild animal. Harmless to humans, anyway.

The relief, while it lasted, was wonderful.

Unfortunately, there's nothing like isolation, darkness and cold for making relief wear off.

"I wonder what frightened it," said Ruth, all too casually.

"Us!" I said firmly. "Just us. There's nothing else here, all right?"

"Not even a tour bus," said Ruth. "They're not going to show, are they? Maybe this Phantom Freebie really *is* a phantom. What do you say we hitch a ride?"

"I say no."

"Why? We have to do something. Or do you plan to settle here for the rest of your life?"

"We may have to do something," I said, "but I am not hitching. I don't want to become a Shock Horror headline in the paper."

"As far as I can see, we're already in the opening credits of a horror movie," said Ruth. "And we'd pick carefully. We wouldn't take a ride from anyone dodgy."

"How would we know? Are we going to say, 'Excuse me, are you a psychopath? No? Oh good. Well will you please drive us along a few lonely Highland roads to a haunted castle. Thank you very much'."

"Yes," said Ruth, "I see what you mean. The background music does get kind of spooky at that point. I just thought maybe we could pick a truck with a really small driver. One we could definitely overpower."

"They'll be here," I said. "They've probably been delayed by heavy traffic or something."

"Well, hey," said Ruth, "it's certainly been like the freeway in rush hour along here in the past hour."

I felt the need to get back in control of the situation. "Listen," I said, "when we meet up with these people, don't let on we have anything to do with the travel business, all right?"

"If you say so."

"If we do, they might start expecting us to do stuff for them. Remember Paris? We're just tourists like them, yes?"

"Fine," said Ruth, "but won't Mr MacCanada give us away?"

"He doesn't arrive until tomorrow night. For tonight and tomorrow until about six, we're incognito."

"So our troubles don't start for twenty four hours. That's nice."

"He won't be any trouble. We hardly have to do anything for him. Just check out a couple of things, and give him the information, that's all."

"This is me you're talking to," said Ruth. "I've been on Jo-tours before. They always get complicated."

"This one will be very simple and easy," I said.

Ruth put her hand behind her ear. "Listen," she said. "Can you hear wild laughter echoing on the wind? That is the sound of the Fates reacting to your last statement."

"There have been times when you've called me cynical," I said, "but it isn't me, it's you."

"Before we have a fight," said Ruth, "I'd like to make a suggestion."

"What?"

"You don't want to hitch a ride. I don't want to die of hypothermia. Neither of us is enjoying the scenery hereabouts. So let's go for a compromise." She stood up and shouldered her back-pack. "You have the map. Let's walk."

I pulled the fax of the map out of the side-pocket of my pack. "I'm not sure of the scale of this," I said, peering at it in the fading light. "It looks fairly straightforward, but I'd hate to get lost out here."

Ruth didn't answer.

I looked up.

She was already walking down the dim road, jacket hood up, head down.

"Ruth," I called. "The coach could come any second now, you know."

Ruth turned but continued walking. Backwards. "Your decision," she said. "Wait if you want to."

I looked behind me at the blackened empty pub. I looked the other way at the receding, hooded figure.

The decision wasn't a hard one. I struggled to my feet and followed Ruth.

CHAPTER FOUR

Cat's Eyes

It was now officially dark. My diary said so. My eyes said so. Ruth said so.

The road didn't have a pavement, as such. It had a murky ditch and next to that a stony verge. Tufts of damp grass grew out of the verge in just the right places to trip us up.

Ruth has mentioned before that she's got a really good torch at home. Sorry, flashlight. But somehow she never brings it away with her. The one she was using now was slim, elegant and smart. It lit up approximately five square centimetres of the ground ahead. I suppose it was better than nothing, but not much.

Mostly we walked on the road. We just staggered onto the tangled wet edges when distant headlights warned us something was coming.

Annoyingly, we could never see what was coming until after it had gone. It was only as it actually passed us that we could glimpse its shape – and any writing there might be on its side. Not that there was much traffic to worry about. Only two vehicles passed us going our way. Only one came by in the other direction. They were all commercial delivery vans.

"It's a shame they haven't heard about street lights out here," said Ruth, colliding with me for the fourth time.

"It's no use just pointing that torch," I said irritably. "You need to wave it about so it gives us a general picture."

Wordlessly, Ruth handed it to me.

I flashed it about importantly for a while, but that wasn't as useful as I'd expected. The beam created lines of light on the darkness, which hung there for a milli-second before they faded. It was a bit like the effect you get if you brandish a sparkler after dark. I gave up and held it the way Ruth had.

Then I said I thought we might have been better off waiting where we were told to wait.

"I was sick of Ye Olde Inne Cinneration," said Ruth. "It was beginning to spook me. Do you want to check the map again?"

"There's nothing to check. We just keep going for an unspecified distance and then turn right."

"And hope this promised coach picks us up before we die of cold, hunger or fright," said Ruth, quite cheerfully.

I walked on ahead, in silence, thinking that this was *not* the best bit of the holiday. At least, I certainly hoped it wasn't.

"Maybe we've got it all wrong," came Ruth's voice from behind me. "Maybe we shouldn't be watching out for a motor-bus with headlights. Maybe we should be listening for the sound of horses hooves and the crack of the whip as the headless coachman

urges them on! Maybe the only light will come from
their flaming red eyes and eerie luminous breath!"

Usually, Ruth's jokes work for me. But not that
one. There was something about the darkness, the
loneliness, the strangeness of that empty Highland
road that numbed my rational mind. If really pushed,
I was afraid I could actually begin to believe in her
fantasy.

"Give it a rest," I said, more snappishly than I
meant.

"Wouldn't that be great, though?" said Ruth. "A
spectral coach driven by a team of night-mares!"

"I'm glad *someone*'s enjoying herself," I said, duck-
ing under a low hanging branch.

"Hnff!" said Ruth, who was immediately behind
me and hadn't noticed the branch.

Before she had time to complain that I hadn't
warned her about it, we arrived at a place where the
road forked.

"This can't be it, can it?" said Ruth. "We've only
been walking for about ten minutes."

I waved the torch beam around until I found a
rectangular sign, set only about two feet from the
ground. 'Inverhaig Castle Hotel', it said. It pointed
to the right.

"This is it," said Ruth, following me round the
turning.

We were on a completely different sort of road.
Narrower, with enormous, dark, dripping rhododendron bushes along each side of it.

"Hey!" said Ruth. "This is the hotel driveway! Do
you realise we sat outside that gruesome pile for
nearly an hour – and we were almost here!"

"I do," I said grimly. "That's another mark against Tumbleweed."

The drive was long and curved, so we plodded along it for some time before we saw anything except the shadowy outlines of the rhododendrons.

As we gloomed our tired way around the bend, though, we did see something. Something amazing. The castle itself.

To be exact, we couldn't see all of it at first. Just part of a great stone wall, with a castellated top and dimly-lit, narrow windows. The rest of the frontage came into view gradually as we got near the end of the great avenue of shrubbery.

Ruth said something very like "Hnff," again, but this time she sounded impressed.

It was a small castle, but big enough to be very impressive. It was built in an L-shape and we could see that though most of it looked strong and solid, there were broken, crumbly sections at the far end on each side.

There was also some kind of derelict wall just visible through the bushes on our left. The remains of some sort of feed-store or animal shelter, I think. A grey cat was walking daintily along the top of the broken wall as we approached. It glared at us with mad eyes, then dropped down on the other side and disappeared.

At that moment I realised that the very faint roaring sound I'd been half aware of for several minutes was getting closer. A glow of light round the bend behind us confirmed my suspicions.

Realising that, even with Ruth's puny torch, we were fairly invisible, we skipped off the drive. As we stood shivering, with the wet leaves drying themselves on our heads, the Tumbleweed tour bus swept past us and up to the wide stone steps and massive front door of Inverhaig Castle Hotel.

"It's over an hour late!" I said.

"Yet another bad mark!" said Ruth, ripping off a small piece of rhododendron that had hit her particularly hard in the face.

"Wait till we meet the tour guide him or herself," I said acidly. "I shall have a few suggestions to make."

As we emerged from our refuge, the castle door swung inwards, and light shone out, down the steps and onto the circle of gravel where the bus was stopping.

We reached the foot of the steps just as the coach driver opened the automatic door from inside.

The excited voice of the woman in the front seat came to us clearly as we walked past.

"I tell you," she said, "I can *sense* presences here! And I *definitely* saw shadowy misshapen figures in the shrubbery – with enormous distorted heads."

Ruth will tell you I went white and almost fainted. This is absolutely untrue. I may have glanced back the way we'd come. I may have looked a bit surprised. But that's all. It was quite unnecessary for Ruth to whack me with her bunch of wet leaves and say, "It was *us* she saw, you great lemon. I'm not surprised she thought your back-pack was your head! It's obviously where you keep your brains."

We passed the bus without being seen. Everyone inside, passengers and driver alike, were far too busy heaving stuff down from the luggage racks to notice us.

In the open doorway we were greeted by a tall, dignified, elderly woman in a white blouse and a plaid skirt. A tabby cat peered at us from behind her legs.

"Welcome," she said, in a soft Scottish accent. "I am Miss Mary MacLeod. I am the proprietor of Inverhaig Castle Hotel, and I hope you will enjoy your stay." Then her formal manner dropped away from her and she said, "Oh, my dears, you're terribly wet. Come inside quickly."

As soon as we were in the hall, I introduced us and explained what had happened.

"I understand that both the guide and the driver on this month's tour are new to the job," said Miss MacLeod.

"That explains a lot," said Ruth, smiling at her.

I surprised us all by grumbling that I didn't think that was any excuse.

Miss MacLeod was beginning to cast anxious glances at the open door. It was obvious that the first people off the coach would be walking through it any second. Then she turned back to us with a smile. "I'll just show you to your room," she said.

"Give us the key and point the way," I said, ashamed of my ungracious outburst. "We'll be all right."

"If you're sure," said Miss MacLeod. She went into a small lobby off the hall for the key. "Now then, I do know," she said, coming back with it, "that you're from Quest and that you're chiefly here to look after Mr MacDonald, who arrives tomorrow night. There is indeed material in the castle relating to him and his family – but may I show it to you tomorrow morning? As I'm sure you understand, I shall have my hands a little full tonight."

"That's fine," I said, taking the key. "Could I ask you a favour? Would you mind not telling the other guests that we have any connection with a travel company?"

"Of course," said Miss MacLeod. "I can see that will make your life easier. I'll have a wee word with the Tumbleweed team – suggest that they keep the information under their bonnets."

The first of the Ghosthunters were already stumbling in through the door and she moved towards them. Just before she launched into greeting-mode again, she turned back briefly and said, "I shall be inviting everyone into the library in fifteen minutes, for a drink before dinner, and to hear a little of the history of the castle."

Ruth and I hurried into the hall, to get out of the way of the horde of incomers.

That's when we realised that though it might be a small castle, it was certainly a real one. The hall was enormous. Stags heads and crossed swords hung high on the walls. The ceiling seemed to be at least two floors above us. The enormous central chandelier had electric bulbs in it, not candles, but it was so far up that it left the whole place dim and shadowy. I could just about see the massive staircase that led up from it, and the vast oak doors that opened off it.

While we were still standing staring, someone broke away from the gaggle of people at the entrance and hurried up to us.

I found myself facing a tall young man, only a few years older than us, with anxious eyes and hair that looked as if he brushed it with his fingers. He was smiling rather desperately. But desperate or not, it was one of the nicest smiles I'd ever seen.

"I'm Nick," he said. "I'm the Tumbleweed courier. I can't tell you how badly I feel about losing you like that. My plan was to unload everyone and then drive back until I found you. I honestly wasn't going to abandon you, believe me. I just haven't quite got the hang of all this yet, but I'm working on it, *really* I'm working on it."

I heard myself say, as if from a long way away, "That's all right. Don't worry about it."

"You're very understanding," he said. He gave me another smile. This one was both desperate and grateful. Then he looked at the rapidly filling hall, ran his hands through his hair and said, "Oh help. I'd better see if everything's all right." He hurried back towards the throng.

I could only hope he hadn't been able to read my expression as well as Ruth obviously had. "I don't believe you," she whispered. "Charm is no excuse for incompetence!"

Then, seeing him talking to one of his charges and gesturing towards us, she muttered that she'd better stop him right now before he told everyone who we were, and moved quickly towards him.

I hardly took in what she said. I suddenly found myself mesmerised by another cat, black this time, which was sitting on the bottom stair. It was looking with wide, amazed eyes at something immediately behind me. I glanced over my shoulder, but there was nothing unusual there – just an empty corner of the shadowy hall and three blank-eyed stags heads.

I looked back at the cat.

Although I hadn't been able to see anything frightening, it was obvious the cat could. It was rigid, one paw raised, its ears pointing forwards. Then it began to weave its head about slightly, as if whatever was behind me was on the move.

Ruth was still talking to Nick. Miss MacLeod was busy with the Tumbleweed tourists. No one was near me and the scared cat.

I spun round one more time and looked frantically in all directions – up, down and sideways. But it was useless. Whatever horror was there, it was entirely invisible to me.

I turned back just in time to see the cat leap to its feet and race up the stairs, exactly as if it were being chased. When it reached the murky, barely-lit landing, it vanished.

That was the first time I'd really looked up the stairs. So it was the first time I had realised what a long, wide, ancient-looking flight it was. Also how extremely dark it was at the top.

I gripped the key in my hand and clenched my teeth. It's all right, I thought to myself. I won't have to go up there alone. All the bedrooms must be up there somewhere. Everyone's going to have to go up that flight sooner or later.

Somehow, that didn't seem to make me feel any better.

CHAPTER FIVE

Presenting the Past

"I'm not sure I want to be first up these stairs," I said – only half joking – as Ruth joined me at the foot of the flight.

She looked at me in amazement. "*First* up?" she said. "Are you kidding? People have been going up and down these for hundreds of years. Follow me."

So I did.

After a certain amount of wandering, up, down and along, between chilly stone walls and past solid looking doors, we found our room.

It had an arched, latticed window, a bulging chimney breast with an empty fireplace under it, an enormous dark-wood chest of drawers and a dressing table fit for a giant. It was the sort of room where you'd expect a four-poster, but in fact it had quite ordinary twin beds.

There was also a very modern electric convector-heater, which Ruth instantly switched on.

I went to the window. It was too dark to see much, but I could make out some kind of forest not far away, and also the shapes of the distant mountains. Over to the left one or two lights glittered. I guessed they were from a group of houses, perhaps a small village.

Behind me, Ruth was opening doors. "We have two walk-in closets," she said, "but no bathroom. Do they *have* bathrooms in castles?"

"We passed one just along the corridor from here," I said.

Ruth screamed.

It wasn't a loud scream, or a long scream, but it made me turn from the window extremely quickly.

She was sitting on an embroidered stool looking in the long spotty mirror of the dressing-table.

I went up behind her and looked over her shoulder.

"Don't worry," I said. "You haven't developed instant zits. It's just that the mirror's old and the backing's coming off."

"No – it's my *hair*," said Ruth. "I look as if someone just pumped a zillion volts of electrical current through me."

The Scotch mist had done its worst with both of us. Ruth's hair was certainly a bit wilder than usual, but mine had gone the other way. A worse way, in my opinion. Flat, dreary and depressing.

"What about me then!" I said. "I look as if I drowned in a lake a week ago and they only just found me. It's all right for you, your hair's *supposed* to be dramatic."

"Not *this* dramatic," said Ruth. "Not so dramatic I even frighten myself. How long do we have to try and repair the damage?"

"Fifteen minutes. Or that's what she said five minutes ago."

In silent agreement that we didn't want to miss

anything, we did our best. There was a bath towel at the foot of each bed and Ruth put hers completely over her head, to flatten the frizz a bit. I hung head downwards and brushed my hair towards the carpet to revive a bit of bounce.

Then we changed our shoes, put on clean jeans on account of the mud around the ankles of the ones we'd arrived in, and pronounced ourselves as ready as we would ever be.

When we got downstairs again, the hall was full of people.

I had guessed right that they would all be grey panthers. What I hadn't guessed, but should have, was that they were all very well-dressed.

Some of them had obviously already been to their rooms and dumped their belongings. Others were still counting their suitcases and disentangling umbrellas and cameras.

One man in particular seemed to be surrounded by hardware. Miss MacLeod was talking to him and as we got closer we heard her say, "I'm so sorry, but I'm afraid it's a rule of the hotel. We feel the other guests would find it intrusive."

"That's ghost-hunting equipment, I bet," Ruth whispered to me. "Shame they won't let him use it. Could be interesting."

Then Miss MacLeod raised her voice. "Hamish!" she called. "Hamish, Robbie, we need you both."

An extremely old man, in a black suit and black tie, appeared from the back of the hall. He picked up the nearest suitcase and began to stagger off with it. Then as soon as its owners began to follow him, he handed it to a sulky-looking boy of about fourteen who had materialised beside him.

They moved off in procession, the ancient figure first, then the clients, finally the boy and the bags. It was impossible not to notice that the old man looked very much like an extra from an early horror movie.

After a short while, he and the boy reappeared and repeated the process.

"He should have opened the front door," I said to Ruth. "Very slowly. And it should have creaked. Very loudly."

Ruth just said, "Hm."

"Don't you think?" I said.

"I think I'm not sure they should employ him at all," said Ruth. "They're using the fact that he's old and stooped. I'm not sure that's okay."

Before I had time to say anything, a small woman with tight grey curls came bustling up and introduced herself as Ellie Proctor.

It was immediately obvious that she had decided to look after the newcomers – us. "Our lovely Nick tells us you're joining us for two days," she said. "I'm sure you'll have a nice time. We're a very friendly group. Now – tell me all about yourselves."

I may have been tired, I may have been surprised by her sudden approach, but I remembered my plan. I was cautious. I gave her our names and told her that we were travelling in the area. Nothing else. Ruth stayed silent and enigmatic.

When she realised we weren't going to say any more, Ellie P let rip. "Now, then," she said, "let me see – Nick you know, and over there is Miss Sommerville," she lowered her voice slightly. "She's travelling free because she made a complaint about some other Tumbleweed Tour. I think she's tense because her firm has just made her redundant. She told me that in confidence, so I know you won't let it go further. Are you both out at work, or are you still studying?"

"Oh well," I said, "You know how it is." And I shrugged.

Ellie waited to see if I'd say any more and then went on. "That couple walking upstairs, Mr and Mrs Norris, he's just retired and finding it hard to come to terms with leisure, don't let them know I've told you this but personally I feel his retirement is putting a serious strain on the marriage . . . I expect you two girls are still single, aren't you?"

Ruth smiled at her and cast her eyes upwards, as if conveying some great truth. We began to move away from her. By now it had gone beyond not wanting her to know we had connections with the travel business. It had become a matter of honour not to give way to her interrogation.

Ellie looked briefly thoughtful, then closed in on us again and continued, "Now the lady over there, you see? – Mrs Willis – she believes she has psychic powers but her husband isn't at all convinced . . . I'm afraid they've been having some quite serious arguments about it. It's unusual for people to join a tour just for two days, isn't it? Do you have some special interest in this castle?"

"We're interested in everything," I said, backing and wondering where we could go that she wouldn't follow.

Ellie reached out and caught my arm. She smiled

to make it seem like a friendly gesture. I knew better, though. I knew we were her prey and she was not going to let us escape easily.

"The gentleman with the heat-seeking cameras and the machine that detects spectral currents in the air is *most* interesting," she went on, "although I'm afraid he's recently had a rather tricky operation . . ."

The only good thing about her, I realised, was that it was impossible to feel nervous about shadows and unseen presences while she was yammering on.

She tried everything she could think of to get us talking. How old were we – did red hair run in Ruth's family – did either of us have relatives in Scotland – who had given Ruth her unusual bear's claw pendant? I nearly cracked at that. I nearly said it was a fossilised shark's tooth and that Ruth's brother George had saved up for it for months. But then Ruth said, "A friend," and I stopped myself.

Even when, guided by Miss MacLeod, we all began to wander into the library, Ellie P was still talking.

The library was nearly as big as the hall. The walls were covered with bookshelves and family portraits. Leather-backed volumes, the sort you wouldn't dare pick up, let alone read, stood importantly in rows. Stern men in Highland dress stared down at us disapprovingly.

A log fire burned in the enormous grate. A few small lamps with thick parchment shades stood about on side-tables. The effect was warm, but dim and shadowy.

Four cats – two tabbies, a black and a smokey grey – were spooking around all over the furniture.

As we all found chairs and sat down I realised three things.

The first was that Nick the courier was now with a frighteningly pretty blonde, who, so the man next to me explained, was Susie, his co-courier.

The second was that Ruth and I were the only ones in jeans and sweaters.

The third was that she and I had become separated and Ruth was sitting beside Ellie P on the far side of the room.

What alarmed me was that Ellie no longer seemed to be doing all the talking. I was too far away to hear the actual words, but I could see Ruth's mouth moving and Ellie listening intently. I tried to signal to Ruth to be discreet, but she didn't see.

Hamish handed out drinks and menus. As soon as we had all chosen what we wanted to eat later, Miss MacLeod took her place by the edge of the mantelpiece.

"This castle is haunted not by ghosts but by its past," she began.

She ignored the faint sigh of disappointment that wafted round the room, and talked smoothly on.

If her listeners had been afraid she would be soothing, her stories unthreatening, they were totally wrong.

She spoke of clan warfare, of family feuds and of terrible deeds during the Highland Clearances.

She told us about murder, torture and imprisonment in dank dungeons. Her calm, soft voice somehow made her stories extra horrible.

She told us we would see weaponry displayed on the walls of all the main rooms. She talked about narrow-bladed swords and huge double-edged clay-mores, about battle axes and cudgels, about dirks and other daggers. She explained, in some detail, what each of them had been used for.

As she worked her way through the gruesome and complicated history of Inverhaig Castle, she would point to one or other of the portraits and say, "That was in his day," or "Their blood was on his hands."

The oil-painted eyes stared back down at us, some of them looking almost alive in the firelight.

She lingered longest on the Ninth Laird whose picture hung above the fireplace.

He was shown full-length, in Highland dress, a sword at his side and – I have to say this – an unpleasant expression on his face. He seemed to be staring straight out of the frame at us.

He looked as if he'd really despised the artist and planned to swipe his head off the moment the picture was complete. Perhaps he did. From what Miss MacLeod said of him, he was capable of it. He had certainly killed lots of other people, including his own brother.

"He once," she murmured, speaking so softly now that we all leant forward to listen, "ordered an old woman to be burnt to death on the grounds that he believed her to be a witch."

The grey cat was rubbing round her ankles and she stopped and picked it up.

"In fact," she went on, "he probably didn't believe that at all. More likely she had annoyed him in some way and he wanted to be rid of her. She died cursing him – and the curse of fire has lain on the castle and all those connected with it ever since."

She drew a breath. "But . . ." she said.

She paused. The fire crackled. The cat rubbed its head under her chin. Somewhere an old board creaked.

"But," she went on, "he is said to have repented in the end. On his 50th birthday, after a lifetime of brutality and cruelty, he ran himself through with his own sword. The very sword that had hacked its way through the necks and limbs of all he thought of as his enemies. The very sword, indeed, that now hangs above the large sideboard in the dining room."

She put the grey cat onto a corner of the empty mantelpiece. It sat down and began to wash its face.

"Then again," said Miss MacLeod, "his action may have had nothing to do with repentance. He was heavily in debt. He may have taken what he saw as the only way out and died as evil and angry as he had lived."

She paused again, allowed the nervous silence to go on longer than before, and then said brightly, "Ah well, enough of that. Dinner will be served in half an hour. I trust that gives everyone sufficient time."

She smiled at us all and then she and the aged Hamish, in his dusty black suit, left the room.

Everyone began to talk at once. Several people moved a little closer to stare at the painting of the terrible Ninth Laird.

I thought I was the only one who was still looking at the cat. So I thought I was the only one who noticed.

Quite suddenly, it stopped washing and turned to stare at the grim portrait hanging above it. Then it made a small squeaking sound, flung itself off the mantelpiece, and went skittering out of the room as if a pack of demons was on its tail.

CHAPTER SIX

The Sword and the Shadow

"I feel so bad about George," said Ruth, as we headed back to our room after Miss MacLeod's vicious tales.

"Why?" I said. "Is he ill? Why didn't you tell me?"

George is Ruth's half-English half-brother. She has been heard to claim that she only half-likes him, but that isn't true. George is all right.

"There's nothing wrong," she said. "I just wish I could have brought him with us. He'd love all this. He was really into Ghostbusters when he was young."

George is not young any more, you understand. George is almost eleven.

"I haven't time to feel sorry for George," I said. "I have too much else on my mind."

"Like what?"

"Like that we're obviously expected to change for dinner."

"That's going to be difficult," said Ruth. "Are you sure?"

"Why else would they give us half an hour?"

I started hauling a skirt and top out of my backpack. I'd put it in for the evening my father took us out to eat on our mini-holiday. I knew that what was all right for a family restaurant might not be classy enough for a castle, but it was all I had.

"Hold on a minute," Ruth said. "How much are these people likely to dress up? If the women are all going to be in strapless satin with sparkly sprinkles, we'll never be able to compete."

I spread my outfit on the bed. It didn't look too creased. "This is the best I can do," I said. "Come on. You brought your purple skirt, I know, I was there when you wore it."

"You miss the point," said Ruth. "If we do our best and it isn't enough we look like failures. If we stay in jeans we look as if we're too cool to bother with fashion conventions."

I wasn't convinced, but I was tired, so I let her persuade me. "What were you talking to Ellie about?" I said.

"You may find out," said Ruth, and smiled annoyingly.

"Why won't you tell me?"

"If you haven't sussed it in twenty-four hours," said Ruth, "I will."

"What am I supposed to do? Ask her?"

"Absolutely not. You mustn't *do* anything. Just wait and see."

That was all she would say.

Dinner was weird. Weird is really Ruth's word, but believe me, it's the right one for the experience.

The dining room was as big as the hall. In fact it seemed bigger because it had a minstrel's gallery. This was not equipped with minstrels. It was being used as yet another place to display weapons, stuffed animal heads and, for variety, a few battle standards.

There were more of all these things around the walls of the room itself, plus a few extra portraits.

I'm not sure who I found the most unnerving – the painted humans, the living humans, or the dead stags. None of them approved of jeans, I could tell. And the women weren't sparkly. They were tasteful, in black or brown wool. My skirt would have been fine.

We were all seated at a single, astonishingly long table.

Ruth and I sat together.

Techno-man, deprived of his spook-hunting equipment, was opposite.

Nick and Susie were next to him. I really wanted to watch them, to see if they were an item. At the same time, I didn't want anyone to know that I wanted to know. I decided to keep my eyes off them. I'd find out soon enough, and anyway, even if he was unattached, why would he be interested in me?

Also, I had Tom. Didn't I? Tom who hadn't answered my last five letters.

Miss MacLeod, now in a full-length plaid skirt and white ruffly blouse, served the food. She was helped by a terrified-looking girl of about fifteen.

Hamish poured the wine.

I concentrated on eating and eavesdropping.

It turned out I'd been wrong to think I was the only one to notice the strange behaviour of the smokey-grey cat.

"Did you notice how that cat went to Miss MacLeod when she was talking to us about witch-

burning?" came a voice from further along the table.
I recognised it. It belonged to the woman who'd been
frightened by our shadowy misshapen figures in the
shrubbery. Leaning forward for a quick look I realised
she was the one Ellie P had told us was Mrs Willis.
"And did you *see* how it ran from the witch-burner's
portrait?"

"Cats often behave like that," said her husband
calmly. "Don't you remember the one we had when
we were first married? Used to go mad and run up
the curtains every evening sharp on nine."

"There was always something strange about that
house," said Mrs Willis.

"You didn't think so at the time," said Mr Willis.
"I'm not sure we should have come on this jaunt.
You're getting a daft look in your eye."

"I can't *help* being psychic," said Mrs Willis plain-
tively. "It's just the way I am. You remember the
night we arrived at Avebury? And the coach drove
past that incredible avenue of standing stones?"

Mr Willis ate his soup in silence. More or less.

"Well – " Mrs Willis went on, "just for a moment
– I glimpsed a primitive horned figure."

"So did I," said Mr Willis. "It was a cow."

"It most certainly was not. It was a two-legged
horned figure."

"It was the front end of a cow, lit by the headlights.
The back end was in darkness."

"You can always tell when there's a ghost around,"
said Techno-man. "The temperature drops and
there's a definite chill in the air."

"How can you tell?" said Ruth, suddenly deciding
to throw herself into the conversation. "The British

49

never heat their homes properly. There's always a chill."

It was then, when she'd drawn attention to herself, that the peculiar remarks began.

Mr Norris said, with a flirty twinkle, "It's very nice to have you with us, but I'm afraid I'm hoping that you're not going to give us a demonstration after dinner."

Ruth did her annoying private smile again and said nothing.

Miss Sommerville leant forward from the far end of the table and remarked, "I imagine any damage to the rooms will have to be paid for." Then she glared at me and said, "I suppose that's your department."

It seemed to me that I was the only one who had no idea what they were talking about.

I leant closer to Ruth and spoke quietly. "Are you playing a practical joke?" I said.

"Kind of."

"Is the joke on me?"

"Certainly not. Don't be paranoid."

During the rest of dinner there were a few more odd comments, but this time they weren't made directly to us. Things like, ". . . must be rich, so the jeans are just a pose . . ." and ". . . not obviously on drugs, but then I'm no expert . . ."

I could tell Ruth heard, but she just winked at me.

I felt cross and shut out. I decided to ignore the whole thing. Then, just as we were finishing our bilberry pie and cream, something happened that took my mind off all of it.

My side of the table saw it first. But within seconds

the people on the opposite side were swivelling in their seats to look behind them.

From what was said later I know that, at the start, lots of us thought we were imagining it.

It was a shadow. That was all. Just a shadow against the wall.

There were so many shadows in that room that I don't know how it got our attention. But it did and, as we watched, it seemed to move slightly.

That was when I looked behind me to see who, or what, was causing it. So did several of the people each side of me.

We all made the same discovery.

Nothing was causing it.

No one was standing up. Miss MacLeod and Hamish had left the room as soon as they'd dished out the pie, promising coffee in the lounge.

The shadow began to grow and take on a shape. It was vague and blurry – but it seemed obvious it was the shape of a man.

All conversation had stopped. The dining room was totally silent. I'm not sure that I was even breathing.

The shape grew darker and more solid. I looked frantically round the room. Shadows are thrown by solid objects. There had to be something – if not a person, then a curtain blowing in front of a lamp. Or perhaps one of the battle standards had got itself unwrapped.

But the curtains hung still, nowhere near the lights. The battle standards, high on the minstrel's gallery, remained tightly wound.

Mrs Willis put her hand to her chest.

Beside me, Ruth gripped my wrist.

My heart was behaving like a ping-pong ball on a fountain.

With so many people in the room, I thought, surely one of us would have spotted the rational explanation – if there had been one.

Suddenly I understood what the shadow was doing. It was moving towards the Ninth Laird's sword, where it hung on the wall above the vast darkwood sideboard.

For perhaps a second, it covered the sword so totally that the blade was invisible.

Then we all heard a short, sharp hiss – in the air – everywhere and nowhere – and instantly the shadow vanished, as if it had never existed.

As soon as everyone was sure that whatever had been going on had stopped, people began to talk, so rapidly that their voices got all mixed up. I think some were comparing notes about what they'd seen. I think others were trying to come up with physical explanations. I know someone began to giggle hysterically.

All I could hear clearly, though, was Ruth's voice in my ear. "So *now* do you believe in ghosts?"

"Never!" I said, in the strongest voice I could manage. I found I had an absolute conviction that the more people who believed in it, the more power it would have. "I won't believe in ghosts till hell freezes over," I said, trying to stop my voice quavering.

"You're really strong, aren't you?" said Ruth. She sounded impressed.

Most people were on their feet now, but Techno-man was the only one who went right up to the great sword on the wall.

I saw him reach out and touch it.

And I saw him snatch his hand back and stare at his fingers.

"Hey!" he said. "Hey come and look! There's blood on the blade! And it's wet!"

I felt myself shudder and Ruth gripped me harder.

"Oh-oh," she said. "I think I just heard the devil polishing his ice-skates."

CHAPTER SEVEN

Owls' Howls

I was sitting up in bed with my sweater over my nightshirt.

Ruth was sitting up in bed with her sweater over her nightshirt *and* the duvet wrapped right round her. She looked like a large caterpillar.

We were the first to retire for the night, but the conversation downstairs had been making our heads spin. Anyhow it was late and we were tired. We had discussed what we'd seen until we were hoarse, but we hadn't got any nearer to understanding it.

"I'm not sure I'm going to sleep tonight," I said. I hoped Ruth wasn't going to suggest turning out the bedside lights yet.

"I'm not sure I'm ever going to sleep again," said Ruth.

We'd already agreed that one of the strangest things about the evening had been the way Miss MacLeod had reacted when she was called back into the dining room and told about the apparition.

She had been embarrassed.

Although she had been the one to tell us about the grisly death of the Ninth Laird, she quite obviously hadn't wanted to know that the event seemed to have been re-enacted in front of us.

"The lighting in the castle is subtle," she'd said. "There were candles on the table. I think you'll find there are shadows everywhere. I'm so sorry you've been alarmed."

We had all protested. Even Ruth and I had joined in. We'd pointed out that everyone had seen the same shape and everyone had heard the same hiss of pain.

Techno-man made more noise than any of us. "There was blood," he'd kept saying. "There was blood!"

Miss MacLeod had examined the sword for herself. "No blood," she'd said. "Perhaps a little rust. It isn't easy to keep everything as clean as we would like."

"But I *touched* it," Techno-man had wailed. "It was *wet*."

We had all clustered round him as he'd held out his finger for her inspection. Most of us, including me, had seen the small smear of glistening red. But by the time Miss MacLeod had turned up it had dried, and I have to admit that made it very hard to spot.

Miss MacLeod had just pointed out, very gently, that it was not wise ever to touch a blade. Then she had offered to fetch a plaster.

Techno-man had insisted he had not cut himself. Miss MacLeod had said she was pleased about that.

Mr Norris had stared at her and said, "I'm surprised at your reaction. We all know this is a haunted castle."

"Haunted by its history," Miss MacLeod had said firmly.

"Are you descended from the Ninth Laird?" Mrs Norris asked.

"No. The family sold the castle many years ago. I am simply a hotel proprietor."

Oddly enough the fact that she, after all her stories, had dismissed what had happened made the rest of us all the more certain of what we'd seen and heard.

Even Mr Willis was interested. Mrs Willis practically went into orbit.

When Ruth and I had made our escape upstairs, some of them were planning to keep watch all night.

I crawled down the bed until I could reach the chair where I'd left my other sweater. Then I draped it around my shoulders, over the one I was wearing, and crawled back again.

"Are you cold or scared?" said Ruth.

"I don't know the difference any more. I just know I can't stop shivering."

A low moan drifted past outside the bedroom window.

"*Now* what!" said Ruth.

"I think it was an owl."

The moan passed by again, in roughly the opposite direction.

"Owls go to-whit to-whoo," said Ruth. "Even I know that. They don't howl like lost souls."

"I think long-eared owls do," I said. "My father would know."

"I wish he was here," said Ruth. "And not just to identify the bird life. We need someone sensible around. All the others are crazy. Though to be fair,

56

I guess seeing a shadow fall on its sword and bleed is enough to make anyone act a little mad."

"Do you think we could talk about something really ordinary," I said. "That wardrobe's beginning to look menacing. I need to calm down."

"Sure," said Ruth. "Good idea. So when are you going to tell Nick what you think of Tumbleweed Tours?"

"They just made a mistake about picking us up. That's history now."

"Yeah. It became history the minute he smiled at you!"

"It has nothing to do with that," I said. "I think we should remember we were added to the trip very late."

"You can sound really pompous sometimes, did you know that?"

"Be fair. They were doing us a favour. They don't normally pick people up there. Why should they know the inn had burnt down?"

"That's another thing," said Ruth. "The curse of fire is on the castle and all connected with it. The Cinder Inn's not that far away. Do you think there's a connection?"

The owl, or whatever it was outside there in the dark, gave another long, drawn-out cry.

"I don't want spooky talk," I said sharply. "Not till morning. Tell me what you said to Ellie. Why were people making those peculiar remarks?"

"Oh yeah!" said Ruth, cheering up. "I decided to sow a seed of gossip and see how quickly she scattered it. She was fast, wasn't she!"

"But what was it?"

Ruth grinned. "I simply said to her – 'Please don't tell anyone I'm a pop singer travelling incognito.' That's all. I didn't say I *was* a pop singer. I left that to her."

"Ruth! She'll look really silly when it comes out."

"Good. She should learn to keep her mouth shut. Think of all the private stuff she told us about the others!"

Outside in the passage, the floor creaked. The creak seemed to move right through our closed door. Then, slowly, it crossed the floor towards us.

"Good grief!" said Ruth. She reversed up her bed until she was sitting on her pillow.

To my own surprise, I wasn't frightened. "It's all right," I said. "That's where we walked when we came into the room. We pressed down loose boards. They're rearranging themselves. I've known that happen before."

"If you say so," said Ruth, sliding off the pillow again.

"What I don't understand," I said, "is why the others told Ellie so much in the first place. We spotted what she was like. Why didn't they?"

"She'll have been more subtle with them," said Ruth. "Face it – we did look like a pair of dorks tonight. She'll have assumed we'd be easy."

Another thought struck me. "Does she think I'm a pop star, too?"

"Not exactly."

"Go on!?"

"I said every pop star needed a minder."

"Thank you very much. This is getting silly. I know

what we can do. We can mug up on our client, Mr MacDonald."

I crawled down the bed again, hauled up my backpack, and found my batch of faxes.

"Great!" said Ruth. "Tell me a bedtime story."

I riffled through the pieces of paper.

"Right," I said, "this is a copy of Mr MacDonald's original letter. He says: 'Dear Quest Tours, blah, blah blah . . . I am Scottish through the paternal line . . . blah blah . . . my Scottish grandfather, Angus MacDonald, worked as deer-keeper at Inverhaig Castle . . . married my English grandmother, Daisy, in 1900 . . . she became housekeeper at the castle . . . blah blah . . . my father, William MacDonald, was born in 1901 . . . emigrated to Canada as a young man . . . married my mother, Louise . . . Canadian with no Scottish blood . . . blah blah . . . have always felt I took after my father and grandfather. Both my parents died some years ago and now that I am retired I would like to get in touch with my roots. Etc, etc.' So that's the bit he knows already."

"He isn't exactly a full-blooded Scot, is he?" said Ruth.

"Now," I went on, spreading the other faxes out on my duvet. "There are these from Fiona via Bill. A copy of his grandparents' marriage certificate. A copy of his father's birth certificate. A note to say the grandparents were married in the kirk in the village near here."

I pushed it aside. "Don't need that, it says so on the marriage certificate. Also this note to say that Angus and Daisy are both buried in the churchyard. And this note – 'Angus and Daisy lived in a cottage in the castle grounds. Cottage partly derelict but still standing. Possibility of a diary in the castle which could be relevant.' That seems to be it."

"You know everything already. What more could he get on the full tour?"

"Lots. Fiona would check back for several generations. And she'd check other stuff. Schools they went to, houses they lived in, places they worked in. His personal tour would take him to see all those. Even if they didn't exist any more, he'd be shown where they used to be."

"Impressive," said Ruth. "Fiona must have good contacts."

"She could probably get it all from New Register House in Edinburgh. They have parish registers, census returns, all kinds of records."

"So why can't Mr MacCanada check them himself?"

"He could. You're missing the point, Ruth. People like him don't want to do things themselves. That's why they book with Quest."

Ruth leant across the space between the beds and picked up the copy certificates. "There's a lot of information on these," she said, sounding surprised. "So what exactly is it we have to do for him when he shows?"

"Take him to see the cottage in the grounds and the kirk in the village. I think I saw the lights of the village from the window. It's not far."

"Do we rent a car?"

"We can do it all on foot. We'll do a dummy run tomorrow to make sure we take him the shortest way."

Ruth had the two copy certificates side by side on her bed and was hunched over, still wound in the duvet, gazing at them.

"You look like a giant grub," I said.

"Thanks," said Ruth, without looking up. "I assume you know that rich North Americans don't like to walk. Especially rich North Americans who've recently been sick."

"Well, I'll think of something. And I must remember to get Miss MacLeod to show us where this diary is so we can lead him straight to it."

Ruth sat back. "I've found something interesting," she said. "At least I think I have. Maybe you already know this."

"What?"

"Mr MacCanada's grandparents were married in 1900, and his father was born in 1901, okay? Sounds neat, right? But look here – Angus and Daisy were married in November 1900 and their son William was born in February 1901! It must have been a shotgun wedding! Bit of a scandal for those days, don't you think."

I took the copies back from her and looked at them. "No, I didn't know," I said. "I don't think Fiona picked up on it either. I expect she was ordering copy certificates for the whole group at once. Then when Mum told her to hold back on Mr Mac-Donald she must have shoved his stuff to one side without really looking at it."

"I suppose *he* knows?" said Ruth.

"He must!" I said. "Don't you think?"

"It doesn't matter, anyway, however you look at it," said Ruth. "They got married in time."

"Even so – I'm glad there's no chance of Ellie getting wind of it!"

"You know," said Ruth, "I feel badly about Ellie. Tomorrow I shall tell her the truth about me."

"If you must. I suppose it doesn't really matter."

"It'd be wrong to keep it to myself. Ellie would be so fascinated. So would the others."

I looked at her. "What do you mean?" I said. "The truth isn't *that* fascinating."

"Not fascinating!" said Ruth. "Not fascinating that I'm descended in a direct line from the old woman the Ninth Earl burnt as a witch!"

"Don't!" I said, hitting her with my pillow.

Ruth narrowed her eyes and made her voice low and sinister. "I could tell them none of the family had red hair until the night of the fire!" she intoned. "I could say it's been red ever since, generation after generation, in memory of the flames." She went back to her normal voice. "Do you think they'd buy it?"

"You can tell what lies you like in the morning," I said, a bit more fiercely than I meant. "But *do not* talk creepy tonight!"

"I learnt something about you on the walk here," said Ruth. "Your sense of humour is solar-powered. It definitely doesn't work in the dark."

CHAPTER EIGHT

Hamish Issues a Warning

Eventually, tiredness was stronger than fear and we both fell asleep. When we woke in the morning, the light was still on and the faxes were still spread all over the duvets.

Ruth was out of bed as soon as her eyes were open. She snapped on the electric heater, then snatched up her jacket and put it over her nightshirt.

"I *have* to go to the bathroom right *now*! I wouldn't have walked along that hall in the dark for a million bucks," she said.

"Why the jacket?" I said. "It's not out of doors."

"It might as well be," said Ruth, hauling open the creaking bedroom door. "The Scots are exactly like the English. They keep their homes the same temperature as their yards."

We got ourselves together and made it down to the dining room. That was when I discovered that Ruth wasn't all that keen to go in.

"Do you think the Ninth Laird really has gone back to sleep?" she said.

I was truly surprised. "I didn't know you were so scared," I said. "You were joking last night."

"I felt exactly like you did last night," said Ruth. "Desperate to keep the hysteria under control. Don't worry. I'll be okay once I get in there."

We walked in together, shoulder to shoulder, to face whatever we had to face.

The huge room was almost empty. There was no sign of any haunting going on. Just four people drinking coffee at one end of the great table – Mr and Mrs Willis, Mr Norris and Techno-man.

The self-service breakfast was spread out on the giant sideboard, under the Ninth Earl's intimidating sword.

The other four nodded a greeting and carried on talking as we went over to investigate the food.

Ruth lifted the lid on a deep dish and peered in. "Heated wallpaper paste," she remarked.

"You *must* know about porridge!"

"I've heard rumours. This is the first time I've seen the evidence."

We chose bread rolls. In silent agreement I poured us orange juice. I think we both felt a caffeine-hit would be more than our nerves could stand.

"This is by *far* the best," Mrs Willis was saying. "Some of the others had tremendous atmosphere – that house in Cornwall! – the stones at Avebury! – those caves in Derbyshire! – Glamis Castle! – but this is the only place where we've actually had an 'experience'."

"And we all shared it," said Techno-man. "Which definitely authenticates it."

As Ruth and I turned from the sideboard with our plates and glasses, Mr Norris called out, "Come and join us! Most of the others are still in bed. We all kept vigil until dawn – but nothing else happened."

As we sat down I wondered if anyone would say anything about Ruth's musical career, but they were far too preoccupied.

"I tell you something very significant," said Techno-man. "Miss MacLeod was caught out by that apparition last night."

Everyone nodded.

"In my opinion," he went on, "she was looking for a gimmick to drum up interest in the castle and she decided to say it was haunted. Now it turns out there really *is* a ghost, and she can't handle it."

"Absolutely!" said Mrs Willis. "And I think I know why it chose to appear last night. I think it was because there were so many psychically-aware people here."

I found I was swallowing my bread roll in great chunks. I wasn't quite nervous enough to walk out in the middle of my breakfast, but I wasn't enjoying the conversation at all. I would rather have been with people who said it was all a lot of nonsense.

Even sceptical Mr Willis seemed convinced. He'd found a copy of a booklet called *A Short History of Inverhaig*, and he was reading out bits of interest.

"Apparently the witch was burned just over there," he said. He pointed out of the dining room window. "On that knoll, left of the rhododendron walk, just in front of that tall conifer. See?"

We saw.

I drained my orange juice.

"But she wasn't a witch, was she?" said Ruth.

For an awful moment, I thought she really was

going to pretend to be the old woman's descendant. Then I realised she was just interested.

"She was really burnt, though," said Mr Norris. "Barbaric business."

Mr Willis had gone quiet. He was leafing backwards and forwards through the booklet, muttering to himself.

"What are you looking for?" said Techno-man.

"A date," said Mr Willis. "This gives the year of the Ninth Laird's birth and the year of his death, but that's all." He looked up. "He killed himself on his birthday, if you remember? I just thought it might be interesting to know the precise date."

There was a tiny pause. Then Mrs Willis said, "I think we all know that, don't we? I think we all know it was yesterday."

I stood up. "Well," I said brightly, "I think I'll go for a walk."

Ruth followed me out of the room.

"Are you all right?" she said.

"Fine. Sorry, did I rush you? Had you finished?"

Ruth gave me a very straight look. "You *do* believe in ghosts, don't you," she said.

Fortunately, before I had to say anything, Miss MacLeod came smiling through the hall. "Are you ready to see the MacDonald memorabilia?" she said.

We followed her upstairs and almost as far as our own room. She stopped some doors away from it, though, and got out her key. "Here we are," she said.

It was a room about the size of ours, but with no furniture except a table and chair in the centre. All around the walls were bookshelves, stacked with bundles of paper and hardbound manuscript books.

"The castle archives," said Miss MacLeod proudly. "As you can see, there's a lot. Last summer we had a student here for a few weeks, indexing them. He didn't get very far, but he did index the diaries kept by the lady of the house at the time when Mr Mac-Donald's grandparents worked here. So we do know they are mentioned. But I'm afraid I've never got round to reading them myself, so I can't tell you if there's anything interesting to be found."

She went to a shelf, took down a pile of bound notebooks, and set them on the table.

"Miss MacLeod," said Ruth, "what happened in the dining room last night was very dramatic. Wasn't it?"

"I hope no one was seriously upset," said Miss MacLeod.

She took a typewritten sheet out of the front of one of the notebooks and placed it beside the pile. "The index," she said.

Then she went over to the narrow window and signed to me to join her. "Over there," she said pointing, "that's the MacDonalds' cottage. And the kirk where they were wed and buried is in the wee village in the dip. The footpath leads from our drive directly to it."

"I see," I said.

I meant that I saw the cottage and the church. But I also meant that I saw that Miss MacLeod wasn't going to tell us any more this morning than she had last night.

"It's a fine morning," she went on, "but it looks like rain later. Perhaps you'd like to look outside first and come back here this afternoon? You may take the key."

"Thank you," I said, accepting it.

"If you decide the walk to the kirk is too much for Mr MacDonald, Inverhaig has a car for hire. It's a wee bit further by road, but easy to find. And now, as you have the key, I will have to ask you to lock up."

I guessed the lock was tricky and she wanted to be sure I could manage it.

"Curiously enough," she said, as she watched me, "this was once Mrs MacDonald's own room."

"I thought they lived in the cottage," said Ruth.

"Oh yes, indeed. But much later, when she was widowed and very old, they brought her into the castle and moved her into this room. The laird and his lady of that time were very civilized and kind. Not at all like their ancestors!"

I was suddenly aware of a figure in the dim corridor, but it was only Hamish, come to fetch Miss MacLeod to the telephone.

"Hamish knows the castle better than any of us," she remarked. "He's lived here all his life."

Then she hurried away to take her call, leaving Hamish standing.

I felt I had to say something to him – it seemed only polite – but I couldn't think of anything.

So I opened my mouth and said the first thing that came to mind, "Are *you* descended from the Ninth Earl?"

"Och no!" said Hamish. "From them that worked for him. They're no a bad family to work wi'."

"Are you a MacDonald, then?" said Ruth.

"Never," said Hamish. "I'm a MacRae."

"It must be strange for you," I said, in what Ruth later told me was my 'visiting royalty' voice, "now that the castle has become a hotel."

"That disnae worry me," said Hamish. "I'm no bothered by normal guests. Though I'll no pretend I'm impressed by ghost hunters."

"Still – they are all customers," I said brightly. "They all help to keep the castle going."

Hamish glowered. "So I'm told," he said.

"Anyhow, they all leave tomorrow," said Ruth.

"And Mr MacDonald arrives tonight," I said. "He's a normal guest."

We had all three been walking slowly towards the stairs. Hamish was ahead, slap in the middle of the corridor and Ruth and I felt it would be rude to push past him.

When I mentioned Mr MacDonald, though, he suddenly stood absolutely still and turned to face us.

We only just stopped in time and stood rocking a little, trying to keep our balance.

"Mister MacDonald," said Hamish, making the words sound longer and more Scottish than I would have thought possible. "Mister MacDonald. Angus MacDonald's grandson?"

"That's the one," said Ruth, looking faintly surprised at the reaction.

"Ach!" said Hamish. At least, it sounded like 'Ach' to me. "I'd heard he was coming. Foolish. Foolish."

He turned his back again and continued on his way.

Ruth and I looked at each other. Then I sidled

past him and managed to get in front of him just as he got to the head of the flight.

"Why foolish?" I said.

"Foolish to look into the past," said Hamish. "Excuse me, young lady, I must be away down the stairs."

"Do you know something about Mr MacDonald?" said Ruth, closing in on the other side of me.

Hamish shook his head. Later, Ruth and I agreed we weren't sure if he meant he didn't know anything, or just that he wasn't going to say anything.

He clasped one hand onto the bannister rail and began to make his way cautiously down.

When he was about half-way he paused and said, without turning round, "No man should look into the past. Who knows what he might find? Foolish. Very foolish."

We watched as he worked his way down the flight and then turned, away from the public rooms at the front, and set off towards the downstairs back corridor.

"He knows about the shotgun wedding, doesn't he?" said Ruth. "He thinks Mr MacCanada is going to freak when he finds out."

"I hope it's only that," I said. "But I have a horrible feeling he knows something else. Something much worse."

CHAPTER NINE

The Charm Offensive

"MacDonald trail-blazing expedition!" announced Ruth. She shoved my jacket at me. "Let's hit the track before they throw the switch on the Scotch-mist machine again."

Down in the main hall, Nick was being besieged by his charges. I felt really sorry for him.

"The coach leaves at eleven," he said, raising his voice so it could be heard above theirs. Not that they were shouting. Grey panthers don't. But they were all talking at once.

Mrs Willis was saying she had no wish to go any-where else. Inverhaig had all she wanted.

Nick explained it was only a half-day trip, to a loch where a phantom water-horse had once been seen. He guaranteed they would all be back by late afternoon.

Mrs Willis was unimpressed. She said she didn't suppose for a moment they would actually *see* the water-horse, whereas here . . .

At the same time, Mr Norris was demanding to be taken to a bank because he'd run out of cash.

Miss Sommerville was complaining that Inverhaig had no shop and no souvenirs.

And Techno-man was grumbling about not being allowed to use his ghost-hunting kit. "They won't even let us take ordinary photographs!" he said. "Not even in the grounds!"

As we walked by, Nick gave us his desperate smile. Then he ran his hands through his hair and gabbled, "I'll check if our route can pass a bank, I think we can probably call in at a weaver's woollen mill where you'll be able to buy – er – woollens and wovens – and I'm sorry but I did warn you 'no photography' at Inverhaig Castle before we set out . . ."

"Isn't it great," said Ruth, as she closed the immense front door behind us. "None of that's our problem!"

We set off through the grounds towards the Mac-Donalds' cottage.

"Poor Nick," I said. "He was completely trapped."

"You have a dazed look. Am I witnessing love at first sight?"

"No, you're not. But he is attractive, isn't he?"

"Doesn't work for me," said Ruth. "I don't go for the little-boy-lost look. I like boys who look as if they know what they're doing."

I brought a picture of Nick into my mind. "There is something lost about him," I said. "You're right. Lost and worried."

"You want to mother him," nodded Ruth.

"I might possibly like to look after him. I certainly don't want to be his mother! Anyway, he has Susie."

"They may not be an item."

"I bet they are."

"Maybe. Next time we see him I'll ask."

"Don't you dare! That'd be like telling him we're interested."

"You *are* interested! Don't worry, I'll be subtle."

Nick caught up with us as we approached the cottage.

He stopped just short of us and shuffled a bit. "Do you mind if I join you?" he said. He was sort of speaking to both of us, but he was looking at Ruth. "It would make such a change to be with normal people."

"Why not?" said Ruth.

He moved up to walk beside us. Beside her.

"I had to get away for a breather," he said. "Susie's taken the hotel hire-car and gone ahead to check on today's route. That leaves me all alone at their mercy."

"You and Susie are quite alike, aren't you?" said Ruth, ultra-casually. "Is she your sister?"

Very subtle, Ruth, I thought.

Nick laughed. I was certain he knew what she was really trying to find out. "No," he said. "We're colleagues."

Then he spotted the cottage. "Oh look at this," he said. "Isn't it romantic!"

I agreed. I thought it was both romantic and sad. There were holes in the roof, one of the top windows was broken and the door hung crookedly from its hinges. The raggedy remains of a curtain hung in one of the downstairs windows. Perhaps Daisy had made it herself. You could see there had once been a garden in front. In amongst the weeds I was sure I could recognise carrot-tops, grown long and wild.

Ruth didn't seem to feel the same way.

"I bet they didn't think that," she said. "Tiny rooms, no heating, no sanitation."

"It'll have been cosy when they lived in it," I said. "They wouldn't have expected heating or a bathrom. It'll have been quite normal to them."

"It'll have been beautiful," said Nick, gazing at it.

I'd like to have hugged him, and not just for the obvious reason. I really wanted the cottage to be looked at kindly.

"Listen," he said, "we're off on this loch visit soon. You are coming with us, aren't you?"

Ruth answered because he was speaking directly to her. "I'm not sure," she said. "We've got a bit of research to do."

He nodded vigorously, until a lock of hair fell down over his forehead. I had an almost overpowering urge to push it back for him, but luckily he did it first. "I know you're from Quest," he said. "Trust me to make such awful mistakes in front of professionals."

"It wasn't that bad," I said.

"Not bad!" said Nick, his eyebrows slanting in anguish. "Not bad to leave you wandering about in the rain and the dark? But we got horribly delayed and I don't think we're working from a very good map. *Do* come to the loch. I could use your advice on how to handle them all – I won't give you away, I promise."

I have to confess that I did begin to do a quick calculation in my head – if we went with him, would I still have time to check on the grave and the diaries – that kind of calculation.

Ruth looked at me and raised her left eyebrow. It's our code for 'you decide'.

The calculation had not worked out the way I would have liked. "I'm really sorry," I said, "but we need to keep going."

"I understand," said Nick. He sighed hugely. "This is the first tour I've been in charge of," he said. "I imagine you guessed that! I didn't know people would expect so much."

Before I could sympathise, Ruth said, "They're not that bad, are they?"

"Oh no, of course not," said Nick hurriedly. "Most of them are okay. But there are a few who are upfront all the time. Mostly the Norrises, the Willises, Miss Sommerville and Mr Marshall."

"Techno-man," nodded Ruth.

"I wish you hadn't said that," said Nick. "Now I'm sure to call him that by mistake."

"How do you feel about Ellie Proctor?" I asked.

"Oh, she's no trouble. She's very sympathetic. In fact she's helpful because she seems actually to *like* listening to other people's troubles which lets me off the hook a bit."

"Listens to them," said Ruth, "and then broadcasts them."

He looked puzzled.

"It's true," I said.

"Yes," said Ruth, "I hope you haven't told her anything personal about yourself. If you have we'll all know it soon."

I did notice that Nick looked slightly uncomfortable. But then, I thought, who wouldn't. He went back to his original anxieties. "They want special diets arranged," he said, "they lose things, they get ill, they nag on about wanting souvenirs . . ."

"That's what you're for, isn't it?" said Ruth, unnecessarily harshly I felt.

"Oh of course," said Nick. "Absolutely. I think I get upset because I'm rather bad at it. I've just finished university and I've been used to thinking in a completely different way. I suppose it was more of a contemplative life, really. I do try, believe me, but when they all come at me at once . . ."

"We know what it's like," I said. I felt he deserved sympathy. "We've both had problems in the past and we've never had to deal with as many as you've got. I wish we could come on the trip. Really."

He smiled his nice smile, pushed his hair back again, caught sight of his wrist watch and gave a yelp. "Oh, I have to get back – where does time go? See, this is what happens. I get distracted by something interesting and then I run late!"

He gave a little half-wave, thrust his hands into his pockets and began to jog back towards the castle.

I waited till he was out of earshot, then I said, "Why don't you like him?"

"Because he thinks he's too good for the job he's doing. And because I have no idea what he's like. All we've seen so far has been an act."

"How can you possibly know that!"

"I'm telling you. We've just been on the receiving end of a charm offensive. It's how he gets away with stuff. He just runs his hands through his hair, looks frantic, says he can't help it, and gets instant forgiveness. It's a technique. And it works."

"It isn't like that at all. He knows he's not doing it well and he's genuinely upset."

"See? The technique works."

We walked on into the village in silence.

It was tiny. A few houses, one with the post office in its front room. A pub. The little grey kirk.

I pushed open the wooden gate and we went into the churchyard.

We had planned to split up and search half the area each. It was so small, though, that we walked round it together.

Small and totally unspooky.

It was extraordinary. I felt nervous in every room, every passage, and on every stairway of the castle. I always had the feeling that some shade of the long-dead might leer at me round a corner. But in the graveyard, surrounded by the dead of several generations, I didn't feel threatened at all.

It may have been because the headstones were so simple and solid and serious. They looked as though they'd approve of ghosts about as much as Ruth did. There were no winged angels, no table tombs, nothing flamboyant. Just gravestones, some very old, standing in rows like closed doorways.

The MacDonalds' grave was round the side of the church, near the wall. He had died first. She had been buried with him later, her name and dates added below his.

We stood still for a moment. I think we both felt we'd come visiting and it would be rude to walk away at once.

"That's it then," I said. I had completely forgotten

that we'd been irritable with each other. "Shall we go?"

Ruth nodded. "Sure." She'd forgotten, too.

Inverhaig only served lunch if you ordered it in advance. We hadn't, so we went to the pub.

Inside, we discovered that this pub was not serious about eating. There was no menu, no blackboard chalked all over with Dishes of the Day. Just a gloomy landlord who said he could find us a ham sandwich. Maybe.

In the end he found two, though when they arrived we weren't at all sure *where* he'd found them. Ruth's theory was they'd been in the bottom of his kid's lunchbox for a week.

Afterwards we walked back to the castle.

We were almost there, with the door clearly in sight ahead of us, when Ruth made the discovery.

She stopped dead in her tracks and said, "I've lost my tooth!"

For a second I thought she was talking about one of her own teeth. Then I saw that she was fiddling with the silver chain round her neck. "George's shark's tooth," she said. "It's gone!"

"It may be in the pub," I said. "We'll phone them, and if not . . ."

"No," said Ruth, "I had it when I left the pub. I remember a bit of my hair got caught around it and I pulled it free. It was definitely there then. I have to walk back."

"I'll come with you."

"No, you have to check the diaries. Mark the important bits. It's probably my own fault anyway. The revenge of the Tooth Fairy!"

"I can't let you go back alone."

"Sure you can. It's daylight – I'll be fine."

"If I come too we'll have twice the chance of finding it. George'll be *so* upset!"

"Jo, you know you'll hate me if I stop you getting everything set up for the Visiting Mac. You won't mean to hate me, but you will."

She turned back the way we'd come.

I hesitated. "All right," I said, "but if you can't find it, we'll both look, all right."

"Sure," said Ruth. She was walking slowly away from me, bent double, staring at the ground.

"I hope you find it quickly," I said.

"Thanks. I hope you find some really interesting stuff," she called over her shoulder.

"I'm quite sure I won't!" I called back.

I did, though.

CHAPTER TEN

Digging Up the Roots

The Lady of Inverhaig seemed to have written down
every single thing that happened in her life, from the
moment she woke each morning to the moment she
went to sleep each night.

It could have taken me a month to read through
her diaries. Fortunately, someone called Wallace
MacGregor, a student of Scottish Social History at
the Turn of the Century, had read them before me,
indexing as he went. There was a copy of his thesis
pinned to the index. Not that I read that.

But even though (thank you, Wallace) I only had
to look up entries that mentioned the MacDonalds,
there were hundreds of them. Just how much, I
wondered, did his Canadian grandson want to know
about deer-keeping in the Highlands. Or about the
household duties of his grandmother.

I'd torn some strips of paper out of my notebook
so I could mark a few special pages. Then Mr MacD
wouldn't have to read more than he wanted to. But
it was difficult to decide what was special. Also the
handwriting was hard work.

After about a hundred years, or half an hour

depending how you calculate it, I had only found one piece worth marking.

I got up and went to look out of the window.

Though I couldn't quite see the MacDonalds' cottage from there, I could see the trees that hid it. I could also see the distant figure of Ruth, walking slowly back towards the castle. Beside her, presumably helping her search for the shark's tooth, was someone else. Nick.

I'd heard the coach pull away when I'd first sat down. Nick hadn't gone on the loch visit, then.

I went back to the table. If it had been hard to concentrate before, it was harder now.

Nick had skipped the outing in the hope of spending time with Ruth. I was sure of that. I'd seen the way he looked at her. And it was just his good luck that she was out there alone. Wasn't it?

I knew Ruth wouldn't have made up the story about the tooth. I knew she wouldn't have arranged to meet Nick without telling me. Didn't I?

Just as I know Tom hasn't met anyone else in Sydney. Don't I? I know he only doesn't write because he's bad at letters. His younger sister Melanie, who writes often, has told me so.

So why did I feel so edgy?

The truth is, Ruth would always be straight with me. The truth is, Melanie would never mislead me.

Or would they lie to me if they thought the truth would hurt?

It was cold in the archive room, but it was somehow stuffy as well.

I got up and looked out of the window again. The landscape was empty. I felt a great wave of sadness and agitation. It came rushing over me – and then almost at once it washed away again.

I'm just bored, I thought, bored and fidgety.

That was when I had my good idea about how to research the diaries. By the time Ruth came into the room, not much later, I'd made the discovery.

Ruth was grinning. "I found it!" she said, holding out the tooth, now back on its chain. "I missed it on the way out but I saw it on the way back." She made a face. "And I'm afraid I've been rude to your Dream Guy. I'm sorry."

"What happened?"

"He didn't go with the tour. He left Susie to take them. He saw me out there and followed me. I couldn't shake him. I know you like him, but there's something . . . Anyway, he was doing all his nice-guy-misunderstood bit, and then suddenly he starts talking about the light on my hair and then – do you believe this? – he starts stroking my head!"

I began to giggle.

"Okay, okay," said Ruth, "it could have been worse. But I don't like being touched – unless I want to be. I told him to butt out and rack off. He tried the hurt act, but I ignored him, and eventually he went." She sat down on the edge of the table. "You look very cheerful," she said. "How're you doing?"

"Fine," I said beaming at her. Then I remembered. "Ah. Not so fine actually."

"Boring?" said Ruth.

"At first. Then I found an entry about how Angus and Daisy met. She was English, remember? Well a friend of the laird's, down south, wanted to set up a deer herd. So Angus was sent down for a visit, to advise and get it going."

I found my marker and heaved the book open. "Daisy worked as a maid at the house. Angus met her. They fell in love. I'll read you the last line of the entry – 'I understand he plans to bring her home to Scotland with him.' "

"And he did!" said Ruth. "And they married and lived happily ever after! Mr MacDonald will *love* it."

"I know. I was really pleased. Then after that I kept finding short, dull 'Daisy MacDonald made bilberry jam' kind of mentions. And suddenly I had my brilliant idea. I decided to look up key dates."

"Good thinking."

"First I checked the date of his grandparents' marriage. I found the entry about the wedding – what they wore, what they ate – marked that for special attention."

"He'll like that too," said Ruth. "It's historical."

"I went forward to around the date of William's birth. And here's what I read. Listen! 'I have learned today that my action in sending Daisy MacDonald away to my sister has earned me a rather cruel reputation locally – to part a newly married couple so soon.' And then, a month later," I fumbled through the book to find the right place, "this: 'Angus MacDonald has been announcing that he is to become a father in due time. He is of course a father already. Daisy gave birth at my sister's house two weeks' ago on Wednesday.' "

"That's really sweet," said Ruth. "The Lady of Inverhaig was protecting Daisy's reputation. She sent her away for a while so Daisy and Angus could pretend they didn't get pregnant until after they were married. Now that *is* romantic."

"Yes. But there was a bit more to it than that," I said. "I got interested, so I counted nine months on from the date of the wedding – to the time when the baby would officially be born. There wasn't anything much so I worked backwards and two weeks earlier I found: 'It is now two weeks since I despatched Angus Macdonald to my sister's house to greet his "newborn". How deception spreads once it is started. He is back with us now, bringing news of a son.' "

I glanced up at Ruth to make sure she was listening, and read on: " '*He seems as delighted with the boy as if he were truly his own.*' "

"What!"

" 'Indeed I think he has half-convinced himself that he is. We have decided not to bring Daisy and the child back yet – he will not pass for a new-born, especially as we have suggested that the birth was somewhat early. Daisy is said not to be fit to travel yet.' "

"Oh boy!" said Ruth.

"Exactly. Obviously I started looking at every entry after that. Here's the next key one. 'Daisy has returned with the child, supposedly only two months old. I hope there will not be gossip. She will keep him away from public gaze for as long as possible and discourage visits to the cottage on the grounds that he is weakly and might take an infection. Daisy and Angus are well-liked and I suspect that most folk will choose to believe what the MacDonalds, and indeed I, wish them to.' "

"So who . . .?" Ruth began.

"Wait. I realised I'd missed something, so I went back to the wedding entry and worked slowly forwards. And here it is. The bombshell. 'Angus and Daisy Macdonald came to me today, one week after their wedding, and told me their story. It appears that Daisy had had a brief and unwise romance with the children's French tutor at the house where she was in service. When Angus and she met, she was already expecting a baby. She confessed to Angus as soon as he told her that he cared for her.

'The tutor had already been dismissed for making approaches to another housemaid, and Daisy feared instant dismissal once her situation became obvious. Angus was already so fond of her, that he renewed his offer of marriage, and she accepted. However, a child is due to arrive far too soon after their wedding and they do not know how to proceed.

'Angus was so concerned to preserve Daisy's reputation, and himself such a good worker and loyal friend to the family, that I felt moved to help them. I plan to let it be known that my sister is unwell and send Daisy to stay with her for several months, on the pretext that she needs extra help. I feel sure that once the birth is over, Daisy will indeed be useful around the place.' "

We sat silently for a few seconds. Then Ruth said, "I know this is a feeble hope, but is there any chance Mr MacDonald knows already?"

"No. But I'm sure Hamish does. Think – if William was alive he'd be ninety-one. I don't think Hamish is that old, but he *has* lived at the castle all his life. From what he said, his parents obviously worked here before he did. They could easily have been here when it all happened. I bet there *was* gossip. I bet it *was* talked about locally. And I bet it was still being talked about by the time Hamish was old enough to understand."

"It definitely makes sense of all that 'Foolish to look into the past' stuff," said Ruth. "But Mr MacD may know all this. He'd still want to come here. It's where his grandmother lived and it's where his father was raised. Why are you shaking your head? What makes you so sure he doesn't know?"

"I remembered the date of Angus MacDonald's death from the gravestone." I shifted the diaries about till I found the right one and opened it at my marker.

" 'Angus MacDonald's death was a sad loss to us all'," I read. " 'Most of all, of course, to Daisy, whose son William has just emigrated to Canada. Daisy, in her grief, is racked with guilt that her son does not know the truth about his parentage. I have advised her to leave things as they are. She has no knowledge of the whereabouts of the Frenchman, and Angus was as good and loving a father as any boy could hope for.

'He needed his birth certificate for his entry papers, but as Angus is named on it he will find no confusion there. By the time the boy was five, and wanting to know his birthday, Daisy felt able to tell him the true date. Marriage and birth were in the past, by then, and the MacDonalds held in such affection by all who know them, that it is unthinkable that anyone should raise questions. Since William is never likely to examine his parents' marriage lines I see no reason why there should be a problem.' "

"Oh lady!" said Ruth. "Were you ever wrong!"

"It's awful," I said. "Our Mr MacDonald has come all this way, fired up to find his Scottish roots, and he isn't even Scottish!"

CHAPTER ELEVEN

A Grand Entrance

"I could lie," I said.

I was sitting hunched up on the windowseat of the lounge which, I can tell you, was just as intimidating and just as full of severed animal heads as the hall, the library and the dining room.

The black cat strolled up and looked at me. This time it didn't seem to see anything grisly behind me. It just wanted to be stroked.

"I could tell him the diaries were lost in a fire," I said, leaning down and smoothing its head. "You know – fire, the curse of the castle."

"Miss MacLeod would have to lie as well," said Ruth.

"She might agree. I can ask."

"No you can't. He has a right to know."

"Probably. But why do I have to be the one to tell him?"

"All you can do," said Ruth, "is pretend *you* don't know. Take your markers out of the pages. Just show him the books and the index. Let him make his own discovery, in private."

She was so obviously right that I wished I'd

thought of it myself. Even so, I didn't leap off the windowseat at once.

"I'll leave it for now," I said. "He isn't here yet, and I don't want to go back in that room for a while. It unsettles me."

"How do you mean?"

"I don't know. I just . . . No, I don't know. I will do it, Ruth, but not at once. All right?"

Just then we heard voices in the hall and realised the daytrip was back. Almost at once, the sitting room door opened and people began to pour in. They hadn't seen the spectral water horse. But, judging by the bulging carrier bags, they had certainly satisfied their lust for souvenirs.

"We are looking at people who have shopped," said Ruth. "And how!"

"They must have emptied the weaver's woollen mill," I said.

The ones who noticed us, sitting quietly on our windowseat, smiled in greeting. No one came over to join us, though, which was a relief.

"You have me to thank for that," said Ruth. "They know pop stars aren't interested in tweeds, so they're leaving us in peace." She nudged me. "Look who's just come in."

Nick was sidling through the door, pushing his hair back off his forehead and making apologetic faces at Susie.

Susie gave him quite a frosty look. Then we heard her say, "Why don't you go and check on the time-table for the evening? So people know when they need to go and change for dinner?"

"Absolutely," said Nick. "Hey, Suse, you're not

angry with me are you? I explained why I couldn't come."

Susie ignored him and he shrugged and went out of the room again.

I don't think he'd noticed us in our window alcove. Susie had, though. She walked straight up to us. "You're the one they call Ruth, aren't you," she said. There was incredible hostility in her voice.

"It's my name," said Ruth. "Do you have a problem with that?"

"I'd like a word with you," said Susie.

"Fine," said Ruth. "You pick it."

"What?"

"You pick the word you want. It was your idea."

For a moment Susie looked blank. Then her mouth tightened. She can't have been more than a couple of years older than us, but she managed to look at us as if we were children. It didn't help that we were sitting and she was standing, but it's hard to get up when someone is that close in front of you.

"Very funny," she said icily. "I know Head Office has told us we have to look after you, but next time you want anything will you please come to me and leave Nick out of it."

I suddenly felt furious with her. This was the first time she'd ever spoken to us and she was straight in on the attack. And for no reason at all.

I struggled to my feet – and felt better at once.

"You haven't exactly worn yourselves out looking after us," I said. "In fact you haven't done anything for us at all. *Not* that we needed you to."

Susie ignored me.

"Next time you lose something," she said to Ruth,

"please call the gardener, or the police or your friend here. I don't see why I should look after everybody else while Nick runs around after someone from a rival company who's pushed in in the middle of a tour."

She'd been doing her homework. And getting it subtly wrong.

For the first time in my life I understood what makes people say, "Now look here!" I managed not to, though. Instead I said, in my most dignified voice, "We represent Quest Travel, who sell large numbers of Tumbleweed Tours." Once I had Susie's attention I added, "Or used to, anyway."

To my surprise, Ruth was much softer with her.

"Hey," she said. "Don't take it out on us just because the spook-hunters have been giving you a hard time."

"I'm sorry," said Susie curtly, not sounding at all as if she was. "It's been a bad week. I just wanted to make sure that you know . . ." she hesitated. She was still talking mainly to Ruth. "What kind of relationship do you suppose Nick and I have?"

"Colleagues?" said Ruth.

"Is that what he told you?"

Ruth didn't answer.

"Well, I am his colleague," said Susie. "I am also his wife. So he isn't free, all right?"

"I wouldn't have it any other way," said Ruth.

Susie nodded briefly and stalked off.

"Why didn't you *tell* her he hassled you?" I said.

"She has enough troubles. She doesn't need me to draw her a diagram."

"But she was so – so – she implied that *you* – how *dare* she – "

Ruth grinned. "Stop spluttering," she said. "It wasn't personal. It's just the way she's decided to play it, that's all. Upfront. Warn the competition off before anything can happen."

"But you don't want him!"

"Not even if he came with a lifetime supply of Taco chips, no. But she doesn't know that."

"And, by the way, I admit it, you were right about him. He's a creep. Why didn't I spot it?"

"Because his magic worked on you and not on me. We're attracted to different types. Lucky, huh?"

Nick returned to make a general announcement that drinks would shortly be served in the library again, but this time without any accompanying stories from Miss MacLeod.

It was odd, but his anxious expression, and the lock of hair falling over his forehead, didn't look so appealing now. In fact they looked rather irritating.

We escaped and changed. Whatever Susie might think, I was determined we should make an effort to look as good as we could. For Mr MacDonald. She could persecute her clients if she liked. I prefer to take care of ours.

As we made our way back to the library, Miss MacLeod caught up with us.

"Once the Tumbleweed Tour has gone on its way at noon tomorrow," she said, "I hope we can have a chat. I'd like to explain a few things to you."

"We leave with them," I said. "They're giving us a lift to the station."

"Ah," said Miss MacLeod. "Well, then I wonder

if I might be able to persuade you to stay on at Inverhaig for one more night? As my guests, of course. I would very much like Quest to know that we can function as a perfectly normal hotel."

I admit I hesitated for a moment. I'd been bracing myself for one more creepy night. I wasn't sure I wanted to go through two. On the other hand, it would be very nice not to have to travel with Nick and Susie, even for a few miles.

Ruth, I noticed, was already nodding. So I joined in.

"Excellent," said Miss MacLeod. "Oh, and by the way, your Mr MacDonald has just arrived. He's gone to his room but he'll be down for a drink before dinner. I'll introduce you then."

Ruth and I went into the library and found our own little corner, near the door.

"First Susie – and now I have to face Mr MacDonald," I said. "I wish I'd never come."

"It isn't your fault," said Ruth. "Lighten up."

"I'm responsible for him!"

"You are not!"

"I am."

"Well, okay, maybe just a little bit. But you are definitely not responsible for his family history. Anyhow, think about it. How Scottish would he really be – even if his father *had* been Angus's son? His grandmother was English so his father would only have been half a Scot anyway. And his father married a Canadian with no Scottish ancestors at all . . ."

"That's what he wrote in his letter, yes."

"Well then! He already knows his tartan blood's pretty diluted, doesn't he? His mother had ancestors too, you know. So did his grandmother. This Scottish stuff is only a tiny bit of his story. I bet you he won't care all that much."

Miss MacLeod appeared in the doorway and guided us gently back out into the hall.

"Mr MacDonald's just coming downstairs now," she said.

And he was.

Except that he wasn't so much coming downstairs as making a grand entrance. I got the feeling he was sorry that there were only the three of us there to appreciate him.

He was walking slowly, one hand resting lightly on the bannisters, a beaming smile on his face.

He was wearing a Bonnie Prince Charlie black velvet jacket and waistcoat, with silver buttons – a shirt with a white lace cravat and white lace cuffs – and a kilt complete with silver pin and sporran. In other words, full Highland evening dress.

"Won't care all that much?" I whispered in Ruth's ear.

Ruth sighed. "I guess I MacGot it wrong," she said.

CHAPTER TWELVE

Sounds and Sights

"There's just time before dinner," I said, heading for the stairs.

"We'll need to hurry," said Ruth, behind me.

Mr MacDonald had been very impressed that Quest had sent representatives to meet him. He had been delighted to hear that, next morning, we would take him to the cottage his father had talked so much about, and also to the grave.

Then he'd announced that he'd like to see the diaries directly after dinner.

Luckily it had been easy to abandon him in the library, with a drink in his hand and the entire Tumbleweed Tour to socialise with. This left me with about five minutes to get up to the archive room and take my markers out of the books.

"I feel a bit odd about this," I said to Ruth as we jogged up the staircase under the glassy stares of long-dead deer. "It seems dishonest. Or cowardly. Or something."

"You accidentally intruded on something private," said Ruth. "Now you're discreetly backing off. That's all."

Then, as we walked down the long corridor towards the Archive room, she caught at my arm.

"Listen," she said.

We stood still.

"There's someone in there already," I whispered.

Not only was there someone in the archive room – she was crying.

We stood outside the door, staring at each other, not at all sure what to do next.

The weeping had stopped almost as soon as we'd heard it. The room was now as silent as the cold passage.

"Are you sure it was in there?" I said. "Are you sure it wasn't in the next room?"

"I'm sure it was in there," said Ruth.

She stepped forward and knocked on the door.

No response.

She knocked again.

Nothing.

Then she put her hand on the doorknob and looked at me.

I nodded.

She turned the knob and pushed. The door didn't move. "It's locked," she said.

After a moment's hesitation, I put the key in the lock and turned it. As I opened the door, I thought I heard a sob from inside the room. But it seemed I'd been wrong – the room was empty.

"I'm glad you're with me," I said to Ruth.

I walked over to the table. The diaries were lying exactly as I'd left them.

Before I could do anything, though, Ruth said, "I've just thought of something."

"What?"

"Those key dates you checked out? You missed one."

I think I knew what she was going to say before she said it. But she said it anyway.

"You missed out the date Daisy died. I remember it from the gravestone."

"So do I," I said.

I sat down at the table and sorted through the manuscript books. When I found the right page I read aloud: " 'Daisy died this night. Brave about her illness, but, poor soul, still grieving that she did not tell her son the truth. I wonder now if I was wrong to advise against it.' "

"This was the room they gave her when she was old and ill," said Ruth. "You know what that means, don't you? She died in here, didn't she?"

"Now I'm *not* so sure I'm glad you're with me," I said.

I can't explain what happened next, and neither can Ruth. We were both suddenly full of such a feeling of sadness and agitation that we couldn't wait to get out of there. I slammed the book shut and scraped back the chair. Two seconds later we were both in the corridor and I was locking the door and pushing against it to make sure I'd done it right.

We were actually sitting at the long dinner table, picking up our soup spoons, before we calmed down enough to remember that I hadn't removed a single one of my scrap-paper bookmarks.

We'd chosen the same seats we'd had the night before, at one side of the table, roughly in the middle.

Nick and Susie sat at one end, just about as far away as they could get, which suited all of us.

The Norrises were directly opposite us, with their backs to the sideboard. That meant they also had their backs to the Ninth Laird's sword, which hung above it. I could tell they were finding it hard not to keep turning round to look at it.

Mr MacDonald, who was next to Mrs Norris, was having the same problem. He'd obviously been told the story of last night's shadow over drinks in the library.

Ellie Proctor, on the other side of him, was busy questioning him. Of course.

"Oh yes," he was saying, beaming at her, "eight metres of cloth in this kilt! MacDonald tartan – Macdonald of the Isles – greatest of the clans – Lords of the Isles – tremendous warriors!"

I caught Ruth's eye.

She gave a tiny shrug. "There's nothing we can do right now," she said softly. "Relax."

I couldn't relax. My attention was split between keeping a nervous eye on the sword and a nervous ear on Mr MacDonald.

The trouble was – he was a really nice man. He wasn't boasting about his ancestry, he was excited about it and delighted that Ellie was interested.

And in a very short time, thanks to the efforts of Quest Tours, his bubble was going to burst, his happy dream come to an end. I couldn't bear it. I knew Ruth had been right when she'd said it wasn't my fault. And that it wasn't Quest's fault. And that once he had made the decision to visit Inverhaig he was bound to find out one way or another. But I *still* couldn't bear it.

The soup had been and gone and I was eating something meaty. I'd been far too caught up with my anxieties to notice what was on my plate.

Mr MacDonald noticed what was on his, though. "Wonderful!" he exclaimed. "Haggis! I've eaten it at home, of course, but to eat it in the Highlands is something else!"

"What *is* haggis, exactly?" said Ruth.

I swallowed my mouthful rapidly.

Mr MacDonald pointed with his knife at the brown heap next to his potatoes. "It's kind of like what the English call a sausage," he said. "A savoury sausage."

"Right," said Ruth, eating some. "Like pepperoni?"

Mr MacDonald ate a bit more of his, then he said, "You take a sheep's heart and liver and lungs and grind them up and add suet and oatmeal and onion and seasoning and push the whole lot into the sheep's stomach and cook it." He smiled his happy smile at Ruth. "Of course," he said, "you take the stomach out of the sheep before you do all that."

"Oh," said Ruth. "Not *very* like pepperoni."

With half my mind I heard Mr MacDonald launch into a full description of Burns Night in his home town in Canada.

With the other half I wondered if any of the cats were near enough to help me out with the haggis.

I removed a small piece from my plate – quite discreetly, I thought – and held it under the table to see if there were any takers.

"I think that's a bad idea," said Ruth softly.

"There's only one of them in here, and I'm feeding it already. If you join in, it'll explode."

"Robbie Burns, Scotland's National Poet," Mr MacDonald was saying, "born on January 25th."

"Why don't we just leave it on our plates?" I whispered to Ruth. "Why do we think we have to hide it?"

"We celebrate in the traditional way," Mr MacDonald went on, "with feasting and drinking. I pipe in the haggis myself."

"Out of respect for your client," Ruth whispered back.

"You play the bagpipes!" said Ellie, impressed. "Isn't that very difficult?"

"I had no problems. Took to them at once. In the blood, you see."

I had noticed Mr Norris stare past my shoulder twice, frowning a little as if he was trying to focus on something, but I hadn't looked back. If the Ninth Laird was behind me, now, I really did not wish to know.

Just as we were finishing an extremely rich dessert, which seemed to be made entirely of whisky and cream, he did it again, this time nudging Mrs Norris and pointing.

So I did look back, but the room behind me was empty of people, alive or dead.

Then one or two other people began to look and Mr Willis, beside me, leant towards Mr Norris and said, "What is it?"

All conversation round the table stopped.

"I'm not sure but I think it's a fire," said Mr Norris,

half standing up. "Yes, yes it is. Look. Out there –
out of the window!"

I spun round. He was right. Flames were definitely
flickering in the castle grounds.

There was a general scraping sound as people
pushed their chairs back and stood up for a better
view.

As we watched, the flames leapt higher. Suddenly
there was a column of fire, showing red and gold
against the dark conifer to the left of the rhododendron walk.

"Oh boy!" said Ruth, getting to her feet. "Oh boy!
What now!"

"It's up on that knoll!" said Mr Norris, his voice
loud and shaky.

"You're right!" said Mr Willis. "It's on the knoll
where the witch was burnt."

Mrs Willis let out a shriek. "Look," she said. "Oh
look! There's someone in the flames! Can't you see?
They're burning her all over again."

And she folded onto the floor in a faint.

CHAPTER THIRTEEN

The Curse of Fire?

It was dark. It was cold. It was damp and it was bleak.

That didn't stop us all rushing outside at once, towards the flames that flickered silently on top of the grassy knoll.

Well, not quite all of us, and not quite at once. We hesitated just long enough to see that Mrs Willis was all right, and that Mr Willis, Susie and Nick were fussing over her.

Then the rest of us ran through the great hall, out of the massive front door and across the grass beside the rhododendrons.

The bonfire seemed enormous, nearly as high as the tree, but even as I was stumbling towards it, my stomach twitching with fear and haggis, I noticed two things. I couldn't hear burning and I couldn't smell burning.

I was just opening my mouth to say something about this to Ruth, who was right beside me. But before I could speak the fire vanished.

I don't mean it died down. I mean it went out. Totally.

Everybody stopped and the people at the back bumped into the people at the front. Then we moved forward more slowly.

Obviously no one had a torch, and now the flames had gone it was very hard to see. The lights from the castle windows didn't shine as far as the tree. People held onto each other's arms and told each other to be careful.

Techno-man, right up by the conifer, called out, "Nothing's been burnt here! There's no charring! There are no embers!"

"That's because the fire didn't happen just now," said Mr Norris in a sombre voice. "It happened a few hundred years ago. What we saw was an echo. A place memory."

"This is extraordinary!" said Miss Sommerville.

"This is incredible!" said Mr MacDonald.

I sensed a movement behind me and looked back. I could just see Mrs Willis, walking slowly towards us through the gloom, holding onto her husband's arm. There was no sign of Nick or Susie.

"That was a spirit fire," said Mrs Willis, shakily. "And the figure in the flames was a spirit, too."

I hadn't seen the figure in the flames. Nor had the Norrises or Miss Somerville, but several of the others thought they had, and Mrs Willis was certain of it.

"Do you think this is the anniversary of the witch-burning?" said Ellie P.

Then Ruth caught my wrist and towed me away from the group, back in the direction of the castle door. "That was a set-up, wasn't it?" she said. "Someone's doing all this, aren't they?"

We were both shivering, but in Ruth's case it was only because she was cold.

"I'd really like to think so," I said. "It's beginning to wear me down."

"Let's get inside," said Ruth. "It'd be so annoying to die of cold and get recruited as ghosts by the management. There'll be coffee in the sitting room again, won't there? Let's go get some."

Nick and Susie were already in there. They were sitting on the sofa between the log fire and the table with the coffee tray on it.

The moment we appeared, though, Susie picked up her cup and walked out.

Nick followed her, looking over his shoulder at us with an apologetic grin, and gesturing helplessly at Susie, as if to say it was all her fault.

Ruth stared at him, stony-faced.

I went to pour coffees for the two of us. I was so angry with Nick and Susie, I felt like throwing small pieces of furniture at their departing backs.

"What really *infuriates* me," I said, as the door closed behind them, "Is that Susie ought to be trying to impress me."

Ruth raised her eyebrows.

"Well, all right, not me as me, but me as Quest. If it wasn't for people like my father, people like her wouldn't be in work!"

"You can get your revenge," said Ruth. "You can tell your father they're garbage."

"I'm not sure they are. Their group seems happy enough with them. Listen, I thought you believed this place was haunted – what's changed?"

"I did believe it, kind of. Specially last night. It

really had me spooked. But think about it, Jo. The timing was amazingly convenient – twice! Nothing happens till we've finished dessert and we're about to go through for coffee. Would a real ghost be quite so considerate? And both times it works out that everybody sees it. Doesn't that strike you as suspicious?"

"All right, that applies to the sword-thing last night and the fire tonight. But what about the cats? They can't be in on anything. Twice I've seen one of them really scared. The grey one ran away from the Ninth Laird's portrait. And the black one was frightened by something awful in the hall, when we first got here, something that was invisible to me!"

"I didn't see any of that."

"Well I did. I really did, Ruth. And what about the crying in the archive room? The guests don't go there – why bother to set that up?"

"It could be just a little extra that gets switched on when they know someone *is* going up there. We went up there. Mr MacD will go up there."

"But there was something about that room . . . You felt it too."

"Yeah, but come on! This is a castle! It's old and cold and the decor is all blades and taxidermy. I can convince myself of anything in a setting like this. *You're* the one who doesn't believe in ghosts, remember? Why are you talking as if you do?"

"I don't know. I think I'm just keeping an open mind. Supposing someone *is* setting it all up, who do you think it is? You said something out there about 'the management recruiting ghosts'. Does that mean you suspect Miss MacLeod?"

"No, not her. Look how she reacted to the first apparition. She as good as said it didn't happen."

"Who then?"

"I have no idea. Hamish?"

"He hates the ghost hunters. Anyway, he's too serious."

"You're right. So how about Nick? To give a boost to the Tumbleweed Haunted Britain Tour?"

We looked at each other for a moment. Then we both shook our heads at the same time.

"Too incompetent," I said savagely.

"Though it is odd that he never mentioned the haunting when we met him out by the cottage."

We paused for thought again.

Then, "No," said Ruth. "He thinks he's too good to be wasted on tourists. He wouldn't go to all that trouble for them."

"Susie?"

"Can't see it. And anyway, if it was either of them, why only here and not at any of the other places on the tour?"

"Even if we agree it's not Miss MacLeod," I said, "she must know about it, mustn't she? If it is a sort of hoax. There'd have to be equipment around the place. She'd see it."

Ruth drank her coffee in silence. Then she said, "Okay, if it was permanent equipment she'd know. But what if this is the first and only time it's been done? Someone could get away with it, I bet you. She's always busy – it'd be a cinch to set stuff up when she was occupied somewhere else. Wouldn't it?"

"Possibly. We still haven't come up with who-dunnit."

I had begun to watch the door. The sound of voices in the hall meant that the others had come back from the bonfire-mirage. Any minute now they'd be in here.

"I think I may have," said Ruth. "If we're talking technically achieved effects here, what about Techno-man himself? Pretending to be an innocent tourist but in fact putting on a kind of creepy side show?"

I stared at her. "He was the one who found the blood on the sword, wasn't he?" I said.

"Exactly," said Ruth. "If it wasn't him, then I can't see how the blood got there. But if it *was* him, that would have been easy to fake."

"I think you've cracked it," I said. And I really thought she had.

The door opened and we stopped talking.

"We are obviously here at a most fortunate time of year," Miss Sommerville was saying. "The Time of the Manifestations."

I would probably have decided to have an early night anyway, just to get away from their conver-sation. What clinched it, though, was when I heard what Mr MacDonald was saying.

He had an audience around him of Ellie P and the Willises. He had clearly already told them about his connection with the castle. Now he was saying excite-dly, "My father lost his papers and everything else he owned in a fire! It happened when he'd only been in Canada for a few months!"

"The curse of fire on the castle and all connected with it!" intoned Mrs Willis.

"I know," said Mr MacDonald. "Mrs Proctor here has very kindly told me that story. To think the curse of fire could travel right across the Atlantic!"

"I can't stand it," I said to Ruth on the quiet. "He's going to be devastated. Let's get out of here."

"His father *was* connected with the castle," Ruth muttered. "He may not have been a MacDonald, but he was raised here."

I ignored her and hurried out. She followed.

We had got as far as the foot of the stairs when we heard a voice behind us. Mr MacDonald had followed us.

"Jo," he said, "I'd like to see the diaries now. Miss MacLeod tells me you have the key." Then he added, "Boy, she sure doesn't like having ghosts in her backyard, does she? We met up with her on the way back in, but we couldn't get her to talk about it at all. I'm real sorry I missed her speech last night. From what I hear, she was a bit livelier then."

"She doesn't mind talking about violent death," said Ruth. "Because that's historical. It's the supernatural she can't handle."

"So why does she have a ghost-hunting tour come here?"

"I don't think any hotel would want to turn away bookings," I said.

"I guess that'll be it," said Mr MacDonald. He smiled at me. "The key?" he said.

"You don't want to start researching your past tonight, do you?" said Ruth rapidly. "Shouldn't you get some rest?"

"You think I could sleep?" said Mr MacDonald cheerfully. "The excitement of actually being at

Inverhaig is enough to keep me awake half the night. Throw in a mysterious fire, and that's the other half taken care of."

I couldn't stall any longer. I'd put the key on the chain round my neck for safekeeping. I unhooked it and led the way up the stairs. There was no need for Ruth to come too, but she did, for moral support. I was grateful for that.

There were no strange sounds from the archive room this time.

I opened the door onto pitch darkness and felt a moment of panic as I scrabbled on the wall for the light switch, but it was all right. It was there and it worked.

"Oh," said Mr MacDonald, moving over to the table. "You've marked the places for me. That was very efficient. Thank you."

"There's an index," I said hurriedly, handing it to him. "There are lots more entries about the Mac-Donalds."

Then, finally, I looked him in the eye. "I'm really sorry," I said.

"What for?" said Mr MacDonald, surprised.

"Well – I don't know what to say. Just – I'm sorry."

The smile left Mr MacDonald's face. He sat down in the chair and laid his hands flat on the table in front of him. "I'm going to find something bad in here, aren't I?" he said.

"Come on, Jo," said Ruth. "Time we left. We'll see you tomorrow, Mr MacDonald."

Mr MacDonald nodded. He was still staring thoughtfully at the diaries. He hadn't touched any of them yet.

I put the key on the table. "Could you lock up when you leave, please," I said.

Then we went out of the room and closed the door quietly behind us.

CHAPTER FOURTEEN

Revelations

There was no sign of Mr MacDonald first thing next morning. Or second thing, either.

Ruth and I hung around aimlessly. I knew he probably never wanted to see us again. But still I felt we should be available for him, just in case.

"This is worse than the hauntings," I said. "Thinking of him up there, surrounded by shattered dreams."

"It's even getting to me," said Ruth, "and I like to think I'm not sentimental. Can't we do something to take our minds off it?"

"What do you suggest?"

"I dunno. Pick a fight with Susie? Creep up behind Mrs Willis and make a noise like a Ninth Laird? Tease the cats?"

"I didn't know you had such a cruel streak."

"Well I have. And it gets wider when I'm on edge."

In the end we decided to settle for keeping Technoman under surveillance. At some point, surely, he would have to collect whatever apparatus he'd hidden around the place.

He didn't seem in any hurry, though. He took his

time over his breakfast. He talked with the others in the sitting room. When, eventually, several of them headed for their rooms to pack, he went too.

We couldn't very well follow him. So we put on our jackets and went to have a close look at the knoll in daylight.

We searched thoroughly. We found nothing. No wires in the conifer. No projectors in the rhododendrons.

We were about to give up – well, I was, anyway – when Ruth spotted something. "Hey, hey," she said, "do you see what I see?"

She was looking back towards the castle. And there was Techno-man, loping towards us across the damp grass.

"Spotted anything?" he said as he reached us.

"Not yet," said Ruth, watching him closely.

He wandered three times round the tree, looking up at its dark foliage. Twice he pulled two branches a little way apart and peered in at the trunk.

We waited for him to extract some kind of remote-controlled hardware. But he didn't.

"I have wondered," he said, as he walked round the conifer for the third time, "if last night might have been some kind of trick. But if it was, it was a very good one."

We kept quiet. I knew we were both working to the same plan. Let him go on talking until he gave himself away.

The plan failed.

He had one more look, shook his head, said, "This is an extraordinary place," and began to lope back towards the castle again.

That was too much for Ruth. She raised her voice
and called after him, "You haven't fooled everybody.
We know what you did!"

Brilliant, I thought. Bluff him into thinking we
know already. That always works. It does on TV,
anyway.

Techno-man stopped, turned, and walked back.
He looked surprised and flustered. "You do?" he
said.

"Yup," said Ruth. "Quite impressive."

"I thought I'd been so discreet," said Techno-man.
"Do you suppose Miss MacLeod knows too?"

"I have no idea," said Ruth.

"Even if she does," said Techno-man, suddenly
defiant, "what can she do? Confiscate the negative?
It's such a stupid rule anyway."

Ruth looked as blank as I felt.

"And I didn't use any of the other equipment," he
went on. "I just took the one. Of the front of the
castle."

"One what?"

"One photograph," said Techno-man, looking
puzzled. "Where did you see me from?" He
shrugged. "Out of one of the windows, I suppose."

I think he went on to complain that if people didn't
want photographs taken they should supply picture
postcards, but I'd stopped listening. I was busy trying
to rearrange my brain to fit in the latest discovery.
We'd been way off. Techno-man was not the ghost-
maker.

Meanwhile, back at the castle, the coach was being
packed up.

Most people said goodbye to us. In fact Nick and

Susie were the only ones who somehow managed not to find the time.

Ellie P was upset not to see Mr MacDonald again. "Such an interesting man," she said, "and I don't feel I had the chance to hear his full story."

Miss MacLeod lied to her so convincingly that I was quite surprised.

"Mr MacDonald left early for a day's walking," she said smoothly. "He asked me to tell you he wishes you all a very good trip."

Then, as the bus began to roll down the drive, she turned to us. "I'm so sorry," she said. "Hamish didn't tell me until this morning. I'm not sure if he forgot, or if he still felt he should keep the secret." She sighed. "He says retirement will kill him," she said. "So what can I do?"

"Keep on employing him, I guess," said Ruth.

"He remembered hearing about the MacDonald scandal when he was a boy," Miss MacLeod went on. "If only I'd known earlier I could have warned Quest well in advance. I assume there was something in the diaries?"

I told her what I'd found.

"Poor man," said Miss MacLeod. "I suppose there's an element of risk in any holiday, but this is a rather unusual disaster."

And then she led us through to the back of the castle and into a room she said had once been the butler's pantry.

"Do sit down," she said.

We sat. And we stared. To say we were surprised would be like saying Niagara Falls is wet.

It was hard to tell if we were in the butler's pantry or on the flight deck of a spaceship.

"Mission control!" said Miss MacLeod proudly.

She pointed to banks of tiny, flickering TV screens. "I can keep an eye on everyone," she said. "Ensure they're in position before I set off any of the effects."

She looked quickly from one to the other of us.

"The cameras are only in the public rooms, of course," she said hastily.

Then she beamed at us. "I do want to thank you both for playing along so beautifully. The regular Tumbleweed couriers are good, too, but I was a little irritated by Nick and Susie. They just sat around looking scornful. If anyone had noticed, that could have ruined the atmosphere."

The grey cat emerged from under the main console, jumped onto her lap and settled down.

"We weren't playing along," I said meekly.

"You fooled us," said Ruth. "Until the fire. Then we began to wonder."

"Really?" said Miss MacLeod, obviously delighted. "Oh how *nice* to have succeeded in convincing professionals."

I was torn between embarrassment at having been taken in – pride at being called a professional – and a faint flickering of moral outrage.

"In a way," I said cautiously, not wanting to be rude, "it's a bit of a con trick, isn't it?"

"No way!" said Ruth, who was looking happy and relieved. "It's theatre!"

"I never actually tell the visitors they're seeing ghosts," said Miss MacLeod, stroking the drowsing cat. "I simply tell the story of the castle – put on a bit of a show – and let them do the rest themselves. The thing to remember is that people on ghost-hunting expeditions *want* to be haunted. They meet me more than half way."

My flicker of moral outrage was extinguished.

"But there must be some sceptics," I said, "who want to catch you out?"

"Indeed. But they don't book themselves onto a two-week tour. They travel under their own steam and only stay for a night or so. I can spot them. And I simply don't switch on!"

"But after that business with the sword . . ." Ruth began.

"The shadow's nice, isn't it?" said Miss MacLeod, eagerly. "It's my newest effect. The projector is in the mouth of the stag's head on the opposite wall. But of course I have to keep a sharp watch on the screen here and switch off quickly if anyone seems about to stand up and break the beam. And then Hamish dabs the stage-blood on the blade when he goes to clear away the bilberry pie. I don't think he approves, entirely, but he's very loyal."

"But when people talked to you about it . . ." said Ruth.

"You seemed embarrassed," I said.

"Oh of course! That makes it much more effective, don't you think? That way people believe they've made their own discovery, which gives them great pleasure. And then sometimes, unconsciously, they develop the theme a little. For example, didn't I hear Mrs Willis say she saw a figure in the flames last night?"

"Yes," I said. "I'm afraid I missed it."

"It wasn't there," said Miss MacLeod. "Even the flames are not terribly realistic, you know. We project them onto the conifer from among the rhododendrons – of course, Robbie has to sneak out and remove the paraphernalia sharpish, in case anyone decides to conduct a search – but as long as I cut them out quickly enough, people seem to be convinced."

"But the cats . . ." I said. "This grey one – and the black one – I saw both of them *really* spooked."

"There are speakers hidden behind several of the stag's heads and one or two of the paintings," said Miss MacLeod. "I can transmit a hiss – some moaning – the sound of distant clan warfare – all manner of things. I don't always do the same show. And I can also transmit sounds so high in pitch they can't be heard by humans at all."

"And the cat's ears pick them up!"

"Exactly. I discovered it by accident when I was first testing the system. It's probable that when the cats are older they won't react so dramatically. Just now they're young and skittish. And as you see," she stroked the grey, and paused long enough for us to hear its purr, "I haven't exactly driven them to nervous breaking point."

"The history of the castle?" said Ruth. "Did you make all that up?"

"I wrote and published it myself," said Miss MacLeod, "but it's all true. After a fashion. That is to say, some of the information comes from stories handed down locally. There may be a little legend mixed with it. As a matter of fact I thought I might have to rewrite it. An inn near here burnt down

117

recently, and I thought perhaps it was in rather bad taste to be talking of the curse of fire. But it turned out it was empty when it went up. It was being refurbished and something went wrong with the wiring. No one was injured, and the insurers will pay, so I decided not to worry."

"So where are the speakers in the archive room?" said Ruth. "Not many hiding places in there."

Miss MacLeod looked at us with her head on one side and a strange little smile on her face. I thought she was challenging us to guess the answer, so I had a try.

"Behind the books and files?" I said.

"Risky," said Ruth. "Unless you can be certain which books people are going to move."

Miss MacLeod's smile widened. "Oh, I'm so pleased for you," she said. "That's a privilege, you know."

We looked at her.

"You obviously heard the crying," she said. "Do you know, that's what gave me the idea in the first place."

"I don't know if I want to hear what you're going to say next," said Ruth.

"That's our real ghost," said Miss MacLeod. "But I couldn't have relied solely on her. She's not at all frightening. And far too rare and unpredictable."

CHAPTER FIFTEEN

Sheep's Entrails

Miss MacLeod fed us Scottish salmon for lunch and told us her plans for our afternoon. She wanted to drive us around the area so that we could take a positive report back to the office.

"I do enjoy catering to Tumbleweed Themed Tours," she said, "but I would very much like Quest to send me some – what can I call them? – normal visitors. I prefer not to transmit ghosts every week. It could become tedious."

She promised to show us moors, mountains, lochs, waterfalls, deer (live ones), birds (likewise), a golf course, and a small, new ski resort.

"The snow has gone from the slopes now," she said. "But it's very popular during the winter season and I understand they have a cinema and disco on the complex."

We would have set out immediately, but there was one problem. None of us were quite sure what to do about Mr MacDonald.

Eventually Ruth and I made a joint executive decision. We decided we'd politely left him alone for quite long enough. It was time to go and knock on his door.

His room, it turned out, was not that far from ours. To get to it, we had to pass the castle archive.

At first, when I heard the muffled voice inside, I was sure I must be imagining it. Then I saw that Ruth had heard it too.

Before we had time to make another decision – this time about whether to stand our ground or run – the door opened and Mr MacDonald came out. He was wearing ordinary trousers and a sweater. No plaid in sight.

"You haven't been in there all night, have you?" I said, horrified at the thought.

"Oh no," said Mr MacDonald. "I did stay quite late, but then I came back again this morning. There was a lot to read. There was a lot to think about." He looked faintly embarrassed. "I expect you heard me just now," he said. "I haven't gone completely insane – I wasn't talking to myself. I was having a word with my grandmother."

"You mean you actually saw her?" said Ruth.

Mr MacDonald looked puzzled. "No, she died many years ago," he said.

I remembered that he didn't know, yet, that the room had been hers. And still was, in a way.

"I know you must have read the story," he said. "So you know how upset she was at the end." His eyes were very bright, as though he might cry if he wasn't careful. "It was so sad," he said. "I wanted to tell her I forgive her. And that I know my father would have forgiven her, too. She died before I was born, but he often talked about her. He loved her very much – and he loved my grandfather – that is, Angus – as well. I know he'd have wanted me to tell her it's all right. We understand."

"That's really nice," said Ruth.

"I don't know why I was talking to her in there," said Mr MacDonald. "I should really go to the grave."

"We'll take you," I said.

"That's perfectly all right," said Mr MacDonald. "I've looked at the little map on the back of the *History of the Castle* leaflet. I can find my own way there."

I nodded and backed away from him.

"Oh please don't be upset," said Mr MacDonald. "I didn't mean to reject your offer of guidance. It's just that there's no need for you to take the trouble."

"I know Quest has led you to a horrible discovery," I said.

"Not your fault," said Mr MacDonald. "Not your fault at all. I confess I have been through rather a lot of emotions in the last few hours, but I'm quite all right now. People are what matter – not nationalities. I had a great family, didn't I? And if I didn't inherit Angus's blood, then so what!"

"But you always pipe in the haggis on Burns Night," I said. "You'll miss all that so much."

"Oh I shall continue to do that!" said Mr MacDonald. "I still feel I have an affinity for Scotland. I shall pack away the MacDonald tartan, now I know that I'm not entitled to it. But I can wear one of the Scots National tartans. That will be perfectly acceptable. Hunting Stuart's a great one, or there's Black Watch, or Caledonian. I shall have me a kilt made up while I'm here."

"Good for you!" said Ruth.

"Yup," said Mr MacDonald. "Ancestor-hunting is a dangerous game. I shall know better than to play it in future."

A little later, when Ruth and I were standing in the hall, waiting for Miss MacLeod to bring her car round to the front door, he passed us on his way out. He was well muffled up and carrying a walking stick.

"Are you sure it isn't too far?" said Ruth. "We can drive you there in the hotel hire car."

"I'm a good walker," said Mr MacDonald. "The doctors in France told me that's why I'm so fit. That's why I got over the chicken-pox so quickly." He looked thoughtful. "You know, that's a thing," he said. "It turns out my grandfather was French – and there's my daughter, living in France. Maybe there's something in that. I think I might look into it next time I'm over there." He waved the stick cheerily and headed out of the door.

"He's off again," said Ruth. "And totally fixated on the male line, if you notice."

"Miss MacLeod's taking her time getting that car," I said.

"I guess the engine's cold," said Ruth, "like everything else. Jo, you look as if you've just heard your future's been cancelled or something. You want to tell me what's wrong?"

"Let's sum up our achievements," I said. "One. We can't really report back on Tumbleweed Tours because we met two new couriers who, according to Miss MacLeod, aren't typical. Two. We've helped a